NO PLACE TO RUN

"Get your hands up and move over a little more into the light. I want to get a good look at you."

Cavannagh raised his arms and rose from his bending position. Stiff from kneeling, he momentarily lost his balance and thudded against the wall.

"No tricks," the voice warned sharply. "Move over into the light like I told you. That's right. Now turn around slow."

Cavannagh turned around to find himself staring into the blue barrel of a Remington .44 held in the hand of William Meldrum.

Meldrum grinned. "Well . . . so it's Corporal Cavannagh of the Northwest Mounted Police. I told you up in Canada that if you ever returned to Montana, I'd kill you."

Meldrum pulled back the forty-four's hammer. "And that's just what I'm going to do . . ."

GREAT WESTERNS
by Dan Parkinson

THE SLANTED COLT   (1413, $2.25)

A tall, mysterious stranger named Kichener gave young Benjamin Franklin Blake a gift. It was a gun, a colt pistol, that had belonged to Ben's father. And when a cold-blooded killer vowed to put Ben six feet under, it was a sure thing that Ben would have to learn to use that gun — or die!

GUNPOWDER GLORY   (1448, $2.50)

Jeremy Burke, breaking a deathbed promise to his pa, killed the lowdown Sutton boy who was the cause of his pa's death. But when the bullets started flying, he found there was more at stake than his own life as innocent people were caught in the crossfire of *Gunpowder Glory*.

BLOOD ARROW   (1549, $2.50)

Randall Kerry returned to his camp to find his companion slaughtered and scalped. With a war cry as wild as the savages', the young scout raced forward with his pistol held high to meet them in battle.

BROTHER WOLF   (1728, $2.95)

Only two men could help Lattimer run down the sheriff's killers — a stranger named Stillwell and an Apache who was as deadly with a Colt as he was with a knife. One of them would see justice done — from the muzzle of a six-gun.

CALAMITY TRAIL   (1663, $2.95)

Charles Henry Clayton fled to the west to make his fortune, get married and settle down to a peaceful life. But the situation demanded that he strap on a six-gun and ride toward a showdown of gunpowder and blood that would send him galloping off to either death or glory on the . . . *Calamity Trail*.

THE SCARLET RIDERS

#2 THE RETURN OF CAVANNAGH

IAN ANDERSON

ZEBRA BOOKS
KENSINGTON PUBLISHING CORP.

ZEBRA BOOKS

are published by

Kensington Publishing Corp.
475 Park Avenue South
New York, NY 10016

First Zebra Books printing: April 1986

Printed in the United States of America

Dedicated to Mary,
for her faith
and encouragement

Chapter One

Narrowing his eyes, Cavannagh watched the horse-man ride cautiously toward him. The horseman was unaware that he was being observed, for Cavannagh had carefully concealed himself between the branches of a tall jack pine, even going to the trouble of removing his bright red coat and replacing it with a fringed buckskin jacket. From his lofty perch he could see the trail all the way down to Montana, where it disappeared into a long, fingerlike coulee, clearly visible through the field glasses he held rock steady to his eyes.

There was something about the rider that stirred Cavannagh's memory, and as he slowly fingered the little center focus wheel, the image in the glasses sharpened. A tall black stovepipe hat sat squarely on the horseman's head, and beneath the hat was a dark unsmiling face. Long black braids hung down over the rider's shoulders, and he wore a black vest, striped green trousers, moccasins, and leggings. An Indian or a half-breed . . . more likely a half-breed, Cavannagh realized.

"I'll be damned . . ." Cavannagh swore to himself as a vision of the man appeared through the swirling mists of memory. It hadn't been more than two months ago, and he'd only seen him at night, in the flickering light of a Sioux campfire. But there was no mistaking him — Dutch Schultz's half-breed interpreter. Now why was a Missouri gunrunner's interpreter acting as lookout for Montana whisky peddlers?

Cavannagh hadn't reckoned on this and the implications startled him. They would have to be careful. This half-breed wouldn't miss much.

Cavannagh lowered his field glasses, looked below, and quietly called to the two red-coated men standing silently thirty yards back. One of them, Constable Akroyd, waved in reply and he and Constable Bennett led their three horses deeper into the trees, well away from the trail along which the half-breed would pass.

When Cavannagh returned the glasses to his eyes, the half-breed was much closer, less than a quarter of a mile away. An evil-looking bastard, Cavannagh thought. They would let him pass, for a mile or so behind him would follow a whisky-peddling outfit, surer than hell, and that was what they were after. If they tried to take the half-breed first, he'd have time to fire the rifle he carried across his saddle and warn the outfit. So they would follow the standard police procedure and wait for the outfit, seize it, and then Cavannagh would ride after the half-breed and arrest him as well. And that, Cavannagh smiled to himself, would please him greatly.

The half-breed was no more than fifty yards away when Cavannagh saw through his glasses two canvas-topped wagons and four horsemen come into view along the trail where it entered Canada from the long coulee stretching south into Montana. They were little more than a mile back. This was going to be a good catch for the Mounties.

Hardly daring to breathe as the half-breed rode beneath him, Cavannagh heard the dull clip-clop of the horse's hoofs on the soft sandy soil of the trail. He knew that if the half-breed spotted him up in the jack pine, or heard him, or even sensed his presence, he would fire his rifle and those wagons would wheel around and be back below the border in a flash.

As Cavannagh watched the half-breed walk his horse on northward, his image grew smaller as he put distance between himself and Cavannagh's tall jack pine. When he finally disappeared around a bend, Cavannagh turned his attention southward again and studied the oncoming outfit through his field glasses.

The wagons came on slowly, each pulled by four horses, a teamster driving each wagon. Riding alongside each wagon were two riflemen, one on either side. They seemed to know their business, and Cavannagh wondered which Indian camp they were heading for to trade their illegal cargo of rotgut for increasingly valuable buffalo robes.

It would take them twenty minutes to reach his spot, so Cavannagh started lowering himself down the jack pine's boughs until he was a dozen feet from the ground and dropped the rest of the way. Then he loped through the trees to where Constables Akroyd and Bennett waited with the horses.

Akroyd, a sandy-haired man of thirty, handed Cavannagh a brass-buttoned scarlet tunic. Peeling off his buckskin jacket, Cavannagh pulled on the tunic and strapped around his lean waist a regulation gun belt. He completed the process by cocking his blue pillbox forage cap jauntily over his right eyebrow and adjusting the thin leather strap around the point of his chin.

As he gave the two constables instructions, John Tarlton Cavannagh looked the ideal noncommissioned officer of the three-hundred-strong North West Mounted Police scattered across a quarter of a million square miles of savage, untamed land in half a dozen slimly manned outposts of the Empire. His one hundred and eighty pounds of bone and muscle were built around a broad-shouldered, six-foot frame. He had strong determined features set in a clean-shaven, wind-tanned face and steel-blue eyes that never flinched when confronted with difficulty or danger. Although he was only twenty-five, he seemed older, for he had already brushed with death more times than he could readily count.

Bennett, a stocky young man, listened attentively, but Akroyd's eyes were riveted to the brand-new gold chevrons on Cavannagh's arm. Akroyd was an "original," one of the first men to sign his name on the roll of the North West Mounted Police at Fort Garry in November 1873, twenty-two months ago, whereas Cavannagh had only been in the force five months and already he was a corporal. Worse, he was an American, and in the opinion of Akroyd, a loyal Orangeman and Ontarian who reverenced the Union Jack, all Yankees were to be viewed with deepest suspicion.

"All right, let's go," Cavannagh finished up, and he and Akroyd moved through the trees toward the trail, leaving Bennett to hold the horses. They heard the rumble of the wagons before the heavily laden vehicles came into sight.

Cavannagh unbuttoned his holster flap. "The moment you see me step out in front of those wagons, you get behind them. If any of those outlaws makes a move for a gun, shoot him. Understand?"

Akroyd nodded.

"Good. Move out."

Akroyd bent forward and crept through the trees paralleling the trail. Cavannagh drew his heavy .45 Adams service revolver and waited.

It took five more minutes for the wagons to rumble to within thirty yards of him. When he judged the moment right, Cavannagh sprang into action and jumped out of the trees, pointing his revolver at the two gunmen riding on the right side of the wagons.

"Hold it right where you are!" Cavannagh shouted. "You're all covered."

One of the horsemen reached for a gun, but a sharp movement of Cavannagh's revolver stopped him. "No — I wouldn't," Cavannagh added.

Surprise showed on the outlaws' faces. Behind them Cavannagh saw Constable Cavannagh's red-coated figure, his revolver covering the two horsemen on the other side of the wagons.

"Get your hands up and slide down off your horses," Cavannagh ordered, watching closely. "You, too, teamsters . . . down off those wagons."

Cavannagh was pleased they had accomplished this mission without firing a shot. That was the way the Mounted Police liked to work. He shouted, "Come on out, Bennett."

The six outlaws stood with their hands up, their eyes sullenly on the muzzles of the redcoats' revolvers. Cavannagh said to them, "You men form a straight line. Now, with your left hands unbuckle your gun belts and let them drop to the ground . . . that's the way . . . now, step back."

"What the hell's this all about?" grumbled the outlaw who had started reaching for his weapon. A droopy-moustached man of about forty, under a wide-brimmed cowboy hat, a belt of rifle bullets over his shoulder, he was a typical Missouri man, a desperado of the plains ready to make a living any way he could. Probably a Civil War veteran. The others were the same type.

Instead of answering, Cavannagh nodded at Akroyd to watch them while he climbed up onto one of the wagons and looked in. The wagon was packed with five-gallon coal oil jars. He picked one up, uncorked it, and lifted it to his nose. He did the same with a second, then climbed back down onto the ground. Constable Bennett came out of the trees with the horses.

Cavannagh faced the droopy-moustached outlaw. "You're under arrest for importing liquor into the North West Territories."

"Fer *what*?"

"Rotgut! It's against the law to bring whisky into this part of Canada. You know that."

"The hell with yew and yore law! Yew red-coated jackasses ain't gonna be round to enforce it much longer, anyways."

"I wouldn't count on that," Cavannagh told him.

"Yew jes' better count on it, redcoat," the outlaw

spat back. "Yew jes' better count on it."

Cavannagh called over his shoulder to Constable Bennett. "Bring the handcuffs over here, Bennett."

Bennett reached into the saddle wallets and, dangling three pairs of black handcuffs, joined Cavannagh. Cavannagh handcuffed five of the outlaws together and put the sixth, one of the teamsters, onto the first wagon.

"He can drive," he told Constable Akroyd. "The second team will follow the first. March those five ahead of you. String their horses along behind the second wagon."

"Where the hell are yew takin' us?" the droopy-moustached outlaw demanded to know.

"Fort Walsh."

"That's a day's ride, damn it! Yew ain't gonna walk us all thet way?"

"The hell I'm not. Get moving. Bennett, pick up their gun belts, unload the revolvers and toss them into the back of the second wagon."

As Bennett moved to follow Cavannagh's instructions, Akroyd turned to the tall young corporal. "What are you going to do, Cavannagh?"

Cavannagh didn't like his tone and was on the verge of telling him so but thought better of it.

"I'm going after that lookout."

"What for? We've got six prisoners and their outfit. We don't need any more."

"I'm going after him."

"What are you bucking for, Cavannagh? A third stripe?"

Cavannagh gave Akroyd a withering look. "*Corporal* Cavannagh to you, Akroyd. Now do as you're

13

damned well told."

Cavannagh took his horse's reins, swung himself up into the saddle, and cantered northward along the trail. After riding for fifteen minutes he reached behind him to the Snider carbine in its leather bucket back of the saddle and made sure it was ready for instant action. He must be getting close to that half-breed now, he reckoned.

The trail followed a shallow valley that meandered along between ranges of rolling hills, brown-grassed under the autumn sun, dotted here and there with clumps of spruce and jack pine. A dozen miles north the hills grew higher, sharper in outline, with groves of gold-tinged poplar and birch covering the slopes. The Cypress Hills. Cavannagh legged his horse to lengthen its gait. He couldn't afford to let that black-hatted half-breed get that far. A man could lose himself in those hills pretty quickly if he took a mind to.

Around the next hill . . . that's where he should sight the half-breed, so instead of staying on the trail, Cavannagh cut up the grassy slopes, skirted a stand of jack pine, and bore down toward the trail around the other side of the bend from over the hill.

A few minutes later, breaking through a half-mile stand of pines, Cavannagh reined his horse to a walk. He could see the trail for a long way, until it disappeared into the heavier green and dappled golds of the Cypress Hills. The half-breed was nowhere in sight!

Cavannagh whipped his field glasses from his saddle wallets and swept the country ahead — nothing! No sign of the half-breed anywhere.

14

"Damn!" Cavannagh swore softly. "Where the hell did that son of a bitch go?"

He walked his horse down the hill until he was back on the trail. Carefully he scanned the ground, but it told him nothing. The half-breed had disappeared, vanished without a trace as far as Cavannagh could see. Perhaps he'd heard something—the sounds of Cavannagh's horse's hoofbeats pounding along the trail behind him. He must have pulled off the trail somewhere and taken to the hills.

And Cavannagh's eyes went up to the pines growing along the hills. That evil-looking half-breed under the black stovepipe hat could be hidden among those pines right now, watching him.

A hot, prickly feeling tingled down the back of Cavannagh's neck, running all the way down his spine.

Chapter 2

Fort Walsh nestled low on the broad floor of a valley surrounded by rolling, pine-dotted hills and bathed in brilliant autumn sunshine. The sparkling headwaters of Battle Creek danced nearby, not far from the western side of the palisade surrounding the log fort. A Union Jack waved imperially from a tall flagpole near the main gates.

It was a pretty sight, Cavannagh thought, as he led his two constables and six prisoners toward it. It was barely three months old—he had helped build it— and to him it was home.

The foot-sore prisoner with the droopy-moustache whose name was Meldrum didn't harbor the same sentiments as he hobbled toward it.

"Gaddamn red-coated British jackasses! Doin' this t' Yew-nited States citizens. Them telly-graph wires back in Montana are gonna hum all th' way t' Washington when I git outta this mess. By tarnation they'll hum."

"Unless you have three hundred dollars apiece,"

16

Cavannagh commented breezily from up on his horse's back, "they won't be humming for a long time."

"Three hunnerd dollars! We ain't got money like thet."

Cavannagh shook his head in mock horror. "Then you'll be in jail until spring."

Meldrum erupted in a further outburst of cursing, which didn't let up until they passed through the fort's twelve-foot-high main gates. A strapping red-coated sergeant with a trimmed military moustache stepped out of the guardhouse over by the flagpole and bounded across the parade ground toward them.

"Guid day, Corporal Cavannagh," the sergeant greeted him in an unmistakable Scots accent as he cast hard, dark eyes over the handcuffed prisoners. "Ye hae brought some guests tac enjoy Her Majesty's hospitality, I see."

"Hospitality — *hell*!" spat Meldrum. "Yew British jackasses are gonna pay fer this."

Even white teeth flashed against the sergeant's deeply tanned face. "Americans, too. Fellow countrymen of yours."

Meldrum's mouth dropped open and he whipped his head around to glare at Cavannagh. "Yew mean thet tall, cool son of a bitch is an American?" he asked the sergeant.

The sergeant nodded. "Aye. Late of Colonel Custer's Seventh Cavalry. A lieutenant, nae less . . . and a graduate of the United States Military Academy at West Point."

17

A baleful expression covered Meldrum's face as he looked back up at Cavannagh. "Blue-belly, huh!"

Cavannagh shook his head. "No. Not that it's any of your business, but I was only fifteen when the war ended."

"Wal, I was there, sonny—all through it. I've killed a man or two in my time. After I git outta here, I'm headin' straight back south 'cross the border, an' yew redcoats ain't never gonna get yore hands on me agin. As fer yew, if'n yew ever return t' Montana an' I hears tell of it, I'll come lookin' t' kill yew. Yore name's Cavannagh, ain't it. I'll remember yew."

The strapping Scots sergeant scowled at the Missouri man. "Ye keep threatening a Mounted Policeman like tha', ye'll nae be going back tae Montana."

Before Meldrum could open his mouth again, a great bellow swept across the parade square.

"What the thundering blue blazes is going on over by those gates, Sergeant MacGregor?"

The Scottish sergeant spun on his heel and toe to face the direction of the bellow. A tall man made even taller by the brass-spiked white helmet on his grizzled head, wearing a crown and four gold chevrons on the lower sleeve of his scarlet tunic and carrying a steel-scabbarded sword at his side, marched along the parade square toward them. Sergeant MacGregor stiffened to attention.

"Corporal Cavannagh's patrol returning wi' half a dozen prisoners and two seized wagons, sirr."

Troop Sergeant-Major Joseph Francis, bemedaled veteran of the famous Light Brigade's immortal

18

charge into Russian cannons at Balaklava almost a quarter of a century earlier, slammed to an earth-shaking halt four paces in front of them. "Whisky peddlers, eh."

"Aye, sirr."

The sergeant-major glanced up at Cavannagh. "Good work, Corporal."

"Thank you, sir," Cavannagh replied, sitting to attention on his pancake military saddle.

"But you better get 'em all away from the main gates. It looks like a gathering for an afternoon tea party."

Sergeant MacGregor cleared his throat. "Perhaps we should mount a guard over the wagons, sirr. We dinna want any of our oon men getting into any of tha' seized grog."

Sergeant-Major Francis fingered a bushy moustache. "If they do, Sergeant MacGregor, they'll join these whisky peddlers in the guardhouse. Get 'em moving, now."

The troop sergeant-major lifted the heel of his sword scabbard a few inches off the ground, swung around, and marched away around the barrack square.

Sergeant MacGregor nodded up at Cavannagh. "Carry on, Corporal," then he wheeled around and headed toward the NCOs' quarters over against the north palisade.

Cavannagh tickled his horse's ribs with his spurs. To the manacled prisoners, he said, "Let's go. You're almost home."

"Home!" spluttered Meldrum. *"Hell!"*

Cavannagh walked his prisoners across the barrack square toward the guardhouse, leaving Constables Akroyd and Bennett to park the wagons behind the quartermaster stores and stable the horses. As he swung down from his saddle in front of the guardhouse, he happened to glance over at Major Walsh's quarters. A man sporting a flaming red beard and wearing a brown frock coat, brown trousers tucked into knee-high riding boots, and a fawn-colored hat stood in the doorway, intently watching the prisoners. Cavannagh briefly wondered whether he was Major Irvine, the new Mounted Police superintendent from Fort Macleod.

Herding his prisoners inside the log guardhouse, Cavannagh unlocked the handcuffs and assisted the guard constable to record their names, descriptions, and personal property. When the six were locked into the cells, Cavannagh left the guardhouse and immediately came face-to-face with Sub-Inspector Fraser, the officer of the day.

"Those prisoners you brought in, Corporal . . . make a complete inventory of everything they had — horses, saddles, weapons, the whole lot. It's all subject to forfeiture to the Crown."

"Yes, sir."

The two canvas-covered wagons stood together beside the quartermaster stores, a log cabin with sloped roof, the same as the fort's other buildings. Cavannagh obtained a couple of sheets of paper from the stores and climbed up into the nearest wagon.

20

The first things he itemized were the guns he had taken off the prisoners. But it was the rifles that drew his attention. There were ten of them, four from the outlaws' saddle buckets and six lying among their bedrolls. A rifle for each man and four extras. Nothing unusual about that except for one thing—all the rifles were identical and brand-new. He picked one up and examined it . . . feeling the balance, working the lever action, sighting along the barrel. Winchester model '73 .44-40 caliber repeater. Yes . . . it was the same . . . the same as one he'd seen just west of the Cypress Hills a few weeks ago. And he'd bet that halfbreed in the stovepipe hat would have one exactly the same.

Cavannagh was still examining the Winchester when Constable Bennett returned from the stables. Looking up, Cavannagh said, "Go over to the scouts' quarters and rustle up Jules Prefontaine. Tell him I want him over here on the double."

Bennett hurried away, leaving Cavannagh with the ten Winchesters and his thoughts. "Strange," he muttered to himself. "Damned strange."

A few minutes later a great black shaggy head poked its way through the canvas opening, " 'ey, *mon ami*," a deep voice boomed, filling the inside of the wagon. "You get back, huh! Look lak you do pretty damn good, *non*?"

Cavannagh grinned at the friendly, bearded face. "Maybe even better than that, Jules. Climb up here. I've got something to show you."

Jules Prefontaine, half-French-half-Cree Mounted

Police scout, hauled his burly, buckskin-clothed body up into the wagon. He wore moccasins instead of boots, a wide green sash with long tasseled ends around his waist, and a pungent odor of woodsmoke accompanied him.

Cavannagh handed him one of the Winchesters. "What do you think of this?"

The *Metis*, a battered plainsman's hat hanging on the back of his neck by its rawhide thong, took the new Winchester, turned it over admiringly, held it into his shoulder, and squinted along the sights.

"What do you think?" Cavannagh asked impatiently.

The *Metis* scout frowned as he levered the action. "Damn good gun. Jus' lak d' guns—"

"Right!" Cavannagh interrupted, finished the sentence for him. "Like the guns Dutch Schultz was running to the Indians over at Medicine Lodge Coulee a few weeks back. They were so new the packing grease was still on them."

"Oui," the shaggy-headed scout nodded, handing back the rifle.

Cavannagh took it, turned it over in his hands again, and stared hard at it. "Now ten more of them turn up, in the hands of men just like Schultz. Identical weapons, all brand-new. Why not a Henry or a Spencer? This is like an organized, uniformly equipped body of men . . . like the army but with Winchesters instead of Springfields."

The *Metis* shrugged.

A furrow lined Cavannagh's forehead. "There's

22

something strange about these rifles turning up here like this, Jules. Something strange indeed."

Sub-Inspector Fraser half sat on the edge of a table in the orderly room, a spurred boot swinging freely, arms crossed in front of his chest. He listened in silence as Corporal Cavannagh told him about the half-breed in the stovepipe hat.

"I would like permission to take Scout Prefontaine and try to find him, sir."

The officer, not much older than Cavannagh, studied the corporal with cold blue eyes. "I fail to see any point to this pursuit, Corporal. It sounds like a monumental waste of time."

"He's part of that whisky-peddling outfit, sir. He's broken the law."

With a white doeskin glove, Sub-Inspector Fraser flicked a miniscule spot of dust from the rich gold cord on the sleeve of his expensively tailored scarlet tunic. The foppish mannerism and air of aloofness irritated the American. It seemed so damned British, although he was sure Fraser was a Canadian.

"He's probably crossed back below the border by now," the sub-inspector said after a moment.

"Perhaps not, sir," persisted Cavannagh. "He might be hanging around to see what happens to his friends."

Sub-Inspector Fraser stifled a yawn. "I'd hardly think so, Corporal."

Cavannagh's jaw took on a determined set. "I'd like

to take Prefontaine and look for him anyway, sir."

A moment's hesitation, then, "No, Corporal."

Cavannagh's temper rose. Damn that star on your collar, you superior mannered dandy, he thought to himself. Don't treat me like an ignorant NCO. I was an officer, too, not long ago. Aloud, he said, "I know what I'm doing, sir. That half-breed should be in jail with the other six."

Sub-Inspector Fraser sprang off the table. "That will do, Corporal!" he shouted, his face flushing.

Cavannagh shouted back. "You don't understand the implications of that half-breed—"

"Silence, Corporal! You're facing a charge of insubordination!"

An inner door burst open. "What the hell's going on in here?"

Major James Morrow Walsh, officer commanding the fort, stood in the connecting entranceway to his own quarters.

Sub-Inspector Fraser and Corporal Cavannagh quickly drew themselves to attention.

"It's this man . . . Corporal Cavannagh, sir," Sub-Inspector Fraser stammered. "He has some . . . er . . . ridiculous notion about riding down toward the American border and trying to find some half-breed who was acting as a lookout for that whisky-peddling outfit he brought in."

Major Walsh remained framed in the doorway, his goldbraided scarlet tunic contrasting vividly against the dark log interior of the room. His intense brown eyes looked out penetratingly at Cavannagh from under a brow topped by a thick mass of wavy brown hair. "Aren't you getting a bit saddle sore, Corporal?"

"No, sir." Actually Cavannagh welcomed the thought of a day or two of post routine, especially so he could visit Miss April Bannister, an Anglican Mission nurse who maintained a nursing station on the post. But right now he wanted that half-breed more.

"Hmmm." Major Walsh ran his hand across his bushy moustache, then glanced at Sub-Inspector Fraser. "Please be good enough to step into my quarters for a moment, Mr. Fraser."

As the door closed behind the two officers, Cavannagh relaxed his stiff military posture and waited. He could hear their voices but couldn't make out what they were saying. After a few minutes the door opened and the sub-inspector, agitatedly fingering his blond moustache, stepped back into the orderly room. Cavannagh straightened to attention.

"You may proceed on patrol and endeavor to locate that half-breed, Corporal. Scout Prefontaine is to accompany you."

"Yes, sir." Cavannagh saluted, waited until the sub-inspector returned the salute, then spun around on heel and toe and marched from the orderly room out into the bright sunshine streaming down on the parade square.

After a few quick preparations for Patrol, Cavannagh was just leaving the NCOs' quarters to join

25

Jules Prefontaine at the stables when he glanced across the barrack square to the log guardhouse behind the flagpole. The red-bearded man he had seen in front of Major Walsh's quarters earlier stood by the guardhouse window talking to the prisoners inside. Cavannagh still didn't know who this man was, but he was certainly not Major Irvine or any other Mounted Police officer, for it was against regulations to converse with prisoners through guardhouse windows.

Cavannagh bounded across the square to the guardhouse. The red-bearded man's back was to him, but he whirled around before Cavannagh reached him, obviously warned by one of the prisoners.

"Good day, sir," Cavannagh greeted politely. "May I inquire as to your name?"

A set of teeth flashed in the red-bearded face. "Michael O'Shaughnessy is me name. And yours?"

Cavannagh noticed the Irish accent but ignored the question. "It's against regulations to talk to prisoners without authorization, which I presume you don't have."

The red-bearded Irishman flashed his teeth again. "Oh! Really? Oi wasn't aware of that."

Cavannagh caught a mocking gleam in Meldrum's hard eyes as he looked out from behind iron bars.

"What were you talking to these men about, Mr. O'Shaughnessy?"

"Oh . . . oi was askin' them how the trail is between here and Fort Benton. Yes, that's roight. Oi'm on me way there and oi wouldn't want to get lost."

"What makes you think they'd know?"

"Well . . . they're obviously Americans. They'd know."

O'Shaughnessy didn't look like a westerner. His face was pasty, without the telltale tan from sun and wind one got riding the prairies. But the man was no dude, Cavannagh knew, for the insides of his knee-high boots were stained greasy black from horse sweat.

"You could have obtained that information from Major Walsh."

O'Shaughnessy laughed. "Well, oi like to get as mooch information as oi can, Corporal . . . er . . ." His eyes strayed from Cavannagh's steely blue eyes to the two gold chevrons on his sleeve. "Oi'm afraid oi didn't catch your name . . ."

"His name's Cavannagh," Meldrum said from behind the iron bars in the guardhouse window.

O'Shaughnessy grinned. "Ah . . . Cavannagh . . . from County Cavan. A foine Irish name."

Cavannagh didn't return the smile. "What's your business at Fort Walsh, Mr. O'Shaughnessy?"

The grin left the red-bearded face as he glanced again at Cavannagh's chevrons. "Oi'll not be tellin' you that, Corporal Cavannagh. Oi've already explained it to your major. You don't have enough rank for me to have to explain it to you."

Cavannagh was sure the Irishman was lying, but he knew he was wasting time talking to him. "I do have enough rank to tell you to move away from this guardhouse, Mr. O'Shaughnessy. And if you don't

27

move right now, I'll move you. I have the rank for that, and even if I didn't, I'd still move you."

The red-bearded man looked into Cavannagh's determined face. A strange light came into his hazel eyes, shaded under his hat brim. "Oi was just leavin' at that," he replied, and turned and walked quickly away. Cavannagh watched him disappear around the corner of the guardhouse.

The trumpeter was sounding evening mess when Cavannagh and Jules rode out through Fort Walsh's east gate and swung south on the Battle Creek trail that led the forty or so miles to the Montana border. They continued on through sunset and into darkness, making camp around midnight beside a small lake, the pointed tops of spruce and pine silhouetted like barbed spears against the moonlit sky. Bright and early at sunup they were out of their blankets, hunched over a crackling fire forking juicy brown beans into their mouths while a pot of strong black coffee boiled.

"I never knew how good brown beans could taste until I came out West," Cavannagh remarked. "Back home in New York it was usually ham and eggs for breakfast. But out here, at six dollars a dozen, eggs are too expensive for me."

Jules snorted. "Huh! Dat not so. You plen'y rich."

Cavannagh laughed. "Rich! What makes you think that?"

The *Metis* wiped a thick slice of bread around his

28

tin plate, sopping up the remains of his beans. "All Americans from dat place New York rich."

"It's not true, Jules. There's a lot of poverty in New York."

"Mebbe so, but you rich. You used to be officer in American army. All officers rich, lak Major Walsh an' dat new officer, Mr. Fraser."

"Mr. Fraser's rich?"

"Sure. 'is papa beeg guv'ment man in Ottawa. Dat's 'ow 'e got 'is commission."

They kicked their fire apart and ground the ashes into the dirt. Just before rolling up his blankets and groundsheet, Cavannagh folded his red tunic and packed it into his bedroll, replacing it with the fringed buckskin jacket he had worn earlier. He caught Jules watching him, a sober expression on his bearded face.

"What's the matter, Jules?"

"De las' time I see you put on dat buckskin, we get into plen'y damn trouble."

"You know how I feel about red coats, Jules. They look great on parade, but for patrol they're too easily seen."

The *Metis* took his cayuse's reins and threw his saddle on the animal's back. Eyeing Cavannagh across the saddle, Jules said, "Blackfoot lak red coat . . . Cree, too. Red coat, 'e save your life once or twice."

Cavannagh tied his bedroll behind his saddle, picked up his Snider carbine, and swung himself up onto his horse's back. "This half-breed we're looking for . . . if he lays eyes on a red coat, he'll hightail it so

29

fast we won't even see his dust, let alone him."

The *Metis* heaved himself into his saddle and they struck out southward. The early September morning was cool and damp from the nearness of several small lakes, and a frost had whitened the grass all around them. Their breath and that of the horses clouded in front of them, but it took only fifteen or twenty minutes of walking and trotting for them to warm up.

They rode much of the way in silence, and before noon they squatted in tall, windblown grass at the edge of a plateau as Cavannagh swept the country below with his field glasses. Despite an hour of this, they saw no movement along the trails, among the gold-flecked birch and poplars or the deep green of pine and spruce, nor any smoke from a cooking fire.

After munching a quick dry lunch of hardtack, they mounted up and rode down the side of the plateau to the trail again. With the passing of another hour, they reached the spot where Cavannagh had intercepted the whisky peddlers. Here they swung around and followed the trail back north. While Jules glued his eyes to first one side of the trail and then the other, searching for the marks of a horse having been ridden off the trail up into the trees, Cavannagh warily scanned the pines for any movement. Once again he had an uneasy feeling that somewhere up there someone was watching them.

They followed the trail until they reached the place where Cavannagh had cut up into the jack pines two days earlier. Jules spotted Cavannagh's track where it ran up the grassy slope, and further on around the bend where Cavannagh had come down onto the trail again. But he saw no track of any other horse.

They turned their horses and rode back southward along the trail to where they started, Jules this time searching only one side of the trail, frequently dismounting to examine the long brown grass. Still finding nothing, they swung around and did the same thing again, Jules this time examining the other side of the trail, with the same result.

"Mebbe you only dream you saw dis fellow, *mon ami.*"

"It was no dream, Jules," Cavannagh replied glumly. "He was real enough, just as real as he was in that Sioux camp that night."

"What we do now?"

"Return to Fort Walsh, I guess. Anyway, Mr. Fraser will be happy."

But on their way back they did sight tracks, toward sundown, crossing the trail from the trees on the east side.

"T'ree 'orses . . . shod . . prob'ly white mans."

"How old?"

Jules climbed down from his saddle and hunched low over the tracks. "Five, mebbe six hours. Dey were no 'ere when we ride by dis morning, dat for sure."

"They must have been made right after we rode by. We would hardly have been out of sight." Cavannagh lifted his eyes to the trees lining the hills to where the tracks led.

"Mebbe dey were even watchin' us when we rode by," the *Metis* commented, following the direction of

Cavannagh's gaze.

"That's what I was thinking, Jules. Let's see where those tracks go."

The *Metis* pulled himself back up into his saddle and they followed the tracks up the slopes, into the trees, and over the hill down to a shallow valley on the other side. The tracks petered out at the edge of a clump of spruce, but they picked them up again on the other side and stayed with them until they rode onto the blackened ashes of a campfire.

But here there were more tracks, coming down from the north. Seven shod horses.

Jules slid down from his saddle and ran his big hairy hands through the campfire ashes.

"Warm," he said, looking up at Cavannagh. "Dey 'aven't been gone ver' long."

Cavannagh pulled his carbine from its saddle bucket, cocked the hammer, and looked carefully around.

"Whoever these people are, they obviously don't want to be seen. Otherwise they'd have stayed on the trail."

Jules frowned at the reddening sky. "An' I t'ink dey goin' to make sure dey not be seen, *mon ami*. It be dark before we follow dem anudder mile. An' by tomorrow morning dey be long gone 'cross de border."

"Search this campsite thoroughly, Jules. They might have left something behind—footprints, food wrappings, tins—anything that might tell us who they are. I'll keep an eye on those trees yonder."

Cavannagh watched the trees a hundred yards away while Jules examined the campsite.

"Dey all white mans," Cavannagh heard Jules say from behind him. "At least, dey all wearin' boots 'cep' for one, an' 'e wear moccasins. Mebbe In'ian."

Cavannagh whipped his head around. "Or a half-breed! Remember—they're all riding shod horses."

Jules grunted. "In'ans sometam steal shod 'orses." Then he resumed searching, until a minute or two later. " 'ey, what's dis?"

The *Metis* bent down and picked from the long grass a white card half the size of a playing card. He walked back to where Cavannagh sat his saddle and handed it to him. Cavannagh eased forward his carbine hammer, took the card, and studied it.

One side was plain but the other bore a colored illustration—two clenched fists grasping the handle of a double-edged sword and above it a bright green shamrock!

Chapter 3

Major Walsh stood ramrod straight beside his desk, hands clasped behind his back, and watched the post's two officers and half-dozen NCOs file into his office and take chairs placed in two rows in front of him.

When they were settled, he cleared his throat, picked up several sheets of paper, and waved them in the air.

"Gentlemen, I have just received dispatches from Ottawa, transmitted from the British ambassador at Washington, advising that United States authorities have uncovered a plot by the Fenians to stir up trouble along the Manitoba-Minnesota border. Now you might well ask what this has to do with B Troop, way out here in the Cypress Hills, five hundred or so miles away."

He tossed the papers back on his desk, pausing to note the effect of his words on the faces before him.

"The answer is, of course, very little. Except for one thing. The Commissioner will be obliged to keep Swan River and Shoal Lake at full strength to meet whatever threat this Fenian plot presents. Therefore, we won't get the reinforcements we were promised, which is bad enough, because with only thirty of us, we're understrength to effectively cover the Cypress Hills as well as the Wood Mountain country."

Major Walsh moved around to the chair behind his desk, placed his hands on the backrest, and leaned forward.

"I'll say nothing further on that subject. Of more significance to us is a United States Army buildup for a major campaign against the Indians of the Missouri plains. The Sioux and Cheyenne have become increasingly hostile during the summer and Washington expects the situation to worsen. The army is strengthening its forts in Montana and Dakota, and shipping large quantities of rifles and ammunition to them as part of the buildup. But they're experiencing a problem. Bands of raiders are attacking some of the arms shipments and running them off."

"Indian raiders, sir?" asked Corporal Cavannagh, sitting in the second row behind Sub-Inspector Fraser.

Major Walsh shook his head. "No, Corporal. White raiders. Organized bands of experienced fighting men — men the United States Army would sorely like to have in its own ranks, because they're short of men and can't spare enough to guard the shipments."

The major turned his attention to the others.

"The U.S. Army believes the stolen arms are reaching the Indians and they have requested that we keep an eye open for any Sioux war parties crossing into Canadian territory after clashes with their forces, and that we report, if possible, on the types and quantities of weapons they're carrying."

Silence greeted the major's last words.

Until Sergeant MacGregor's Scots accent broke it.

"Do the Americans hae any suggestions as tae hoo we're supposed tae do tha', sirr?"

They all laughed.

"Perhaps Corporal Cavannagh can advise us," Sub-Inspector Fraser said, turning in his chair to stare at the deeply tanned NCO sitting behind him. "From what I'm learning in the short time I've been stationed here at Fort Walsh, he's supposed to be something of an Indian fighter."

Cavannagh caught the touch of sarcasm in the sub-inspector's voice. There was an air of competitiveness coming from the officer who had the advantage of the star on his collar.

Major Walsh came to Cavannagh's rescue.

"I don't think it's quite fair to put the onus on Corporal Cavannagh, Mr. Fraser. His experiences with the Sioux have been on a somewhat different basis than ours will be. Our job will be to make sure they obey our laws should they cross the international boundary, not fight them."

"Of course, sir," replied Sub-Inspector Fraser quietly, turning his head to the front. Glancing past him to the next chair, Cavannagh was sure he caught an expression of satisfaction on Sergeant-Major Francis's weathered profile.

"There are one or two other matters which I'd like to bring to your attention before dismissing you to your duties, gentlemen. One—we're running low on ammunition, and I want officers and NCOs supervising range practices to exercise restraint on the expenditure of practice rounds. Ottawa has taken steps to get more to us. In my opinion they waited longer than they should have, but . . ."

Cavannagh stopped listening. In his mind's eye he saw ten identical brand-new Winchester repeaters . . . an evil-looking half-breed wearing a tall black stovepipe hat . . . a Missouri desperado spitting out the words, "Yew red-coated jackasses ain't gonna be round to enforce it much longer" . . . and a red-bearded Irishman named Michael O'Shaughnessy.

When Major Walsh dismissed them a quarter of an hour later, Cavannagh's mind was still trying to sort out these facts. After stable parade he sought out Sergeant MacGregor in NCO quarters.

"I've been giving a lot of thought to what the major said this morning, Mac."

Sergeant MacGregor sat on the edge of his bunk filling his pipe. "Aye. I didna think ye had your mind on stables."

"You remember Dutch Schultz?"

The big Scot's head jerked up. "I'll never forget him. He's the only mon who ever tried tae run off wi' my service rifle. Nae in twenty years o' soldierin' all over the British Empire did anybody try tha' before, nae even the Fuzzy-Wuzzies in the Sudan nor the *Patahns* up around the Khyber Pass, an' they were always pinchin' rifles."

The sergeant thrust his pipe into his mouth and handed Cavannagh his tobacco pouch. As he packed tobacco into the bowl of his own pipe, Cavannagh told him about the ten Winchesters and the half-breed in the black hat.

"You remember that first patrol we made together, when the major sent us to investigate Sioux activity along the international boundary?"

"Aye."

37

"When I was in that Sioux camp that one night, I saw half a dozen white men and a half-breed in a tall black hat. The white men were typical Missouri outlaws like those six in the guardhouse. At first I thought they were whisky peddlers, but they were running guns — Winchester model '73 repeaters, identical to the ones I looked at the other day. Of the half-dozen or so gunrunners in the Sioux camp that night, only two are still alive. One is the half-breed in the stovepipe hat, the lookout for the prisoners in the guardhouse."

Sergeant MacGregor rattled his pipestem along his teeth. "And the other is Dutch Schultz. Bit of a scoundrel. I was nae in complete agreement wi' ye in lettin' him go, even though he did help ye in the end. Anyway, I dinna see wha' this has tae do wi' wha' the major was talking aboot."

"I have a feeling there's a connection between Dutch Schultz and those whisky peddlers I brought in a few days ago."

Sergeant MacGregor blew blue smoke toward the ceiling. "That's quite possible. All the more reason ye should hae told the major he was gunrunning. He'd nae be peddling whisky noo."

Cavannagh shook his head. "That's not the connection I have in mind. Schultz is too ambitious to peddle whisky. That's why he was running rifles."

MacGregor frowned. "I may be a little dull, but I *still* don't see wha' this has to do with wha' the major was talking aboot."

"I think there's a connection between the prisoners in the guardhouse and those raiders the major mentioned. Remember, he said *organized bands of experi-*

38

enced fighting men. These whisky peddlers I brought in were all armed with the same weapon, like a stores issue. It strikes me, there's a similarity to a military body."

"Except tha' the Winchester is nae a military weapon."

"For what those raiders are doing, it's better than a military weapon. It's a repeater, which the army doesn't have."

A trumpet sounded from the parade square. Sergeant MacGregor stood up and reached for his pillbox hat. "Aboot time tha' idle trumpeter sounded mess. I'm a wee bit hungry."

Cavannagh ignored the mess call. "Schultz had some good connections because the Winchesters he was running were factory packed and in almost unlimited supply. It would have taken some organization getting them from the factory, across Montana, past army patrols, and over the border into Canada — an impressive display of logistics considering the frequency of army patrols on the plains these days."

Sergeant MacGregor slapped a paternal hand on Cavannagh's shoulder. "I'm hungry, laddie, and when I'm hungry my brain dinna function like it should. I still fail tae see —"

"Damn it all, Mac!" Cavannagh exclaimed irritably. "It should be quite plain. Anyone who can spirit away a few hundred of the most modern repeating rifles in the country can log the movements of army supply wagons and spirit them away just as easily. This is the work of Missouri outlaws and Civil War veterans led by someone with the connections and ambition of Dutch Schultz."

"Hmmm," was all MacGregor said.

"I could find out more about this if the major would give me permission to ride down into Montana and scout around. I never did tell him the full story about Schultz. I'll have to now. How do you think he'll react to that?"

The Scot fixed his hard brown eyes onto the younger man. "He'll hae your guts for tomorrow morning's breakfast!"

With the standard Mounted Policeman's dinner of roast beef and potatoes under his belt, Corporal Cavannagh stood in front of Major Walsh's desk and explained his suspicions as he had to Sergeant MacGregor, and then went on to tell his commanding officer all about Dutch Schultz. That done, he braced himself for a blast, aware of the major's short temper and his reputation for colorful, and sometimes intemperate, language when he got riled. Cavannagh was more than mildly surprised — and considerably relieved — when it didn't come.

All Major Walsh said was: "You should have held him and given me a full report, relying on my judgment to take the appropriate action. Certainly the man would have received some leniency for his cooperation."

Cavannagh's eyes fixed on the embroidered crowns on the collar of Major Walsh's gold-trimmed scarlet tunic, as he waited for the major's next words.

"And you think this Schultz fellow might be behind the raids on American army munitions shipments?"

"He mightn't be the brains behind it, sir, but it's the

40

sort of thing he'd push for someone else."

"This is more a problem for the American authorities than it is for us."

"With all respect, sir, it could very quickly become a Mounted Police problem. Prolonged warfare between the United States Army and the Indian tribes of the Missouri plains could spill over into the North West Territories. If the Indians continue to get arms and ammunition, warfare surely will be prolonged."

"You're quite right, Corporal." Walsh waved a hand at Cavannagh. "Sit down. You obviously had something in mind when you decided to tell me all this."

Cavannagh sat down in a chair opposite the major's desk, leaning forward eagerly. "I would like authority to cross into Montana and investigate, sir. I believe I could find out enough to benefit both the United States government and the Mounted Police."

The major sat back and thoughtfully studied the young, dark-haired NCO. "Where would you start?"

"Looking for Schultz, sir."

"That could be dangerous."

"I'm willing to take the chance."

"Any idea where he might be?"

"He used to hang around Fort Benton."

"A likely spot."

"I would also like to take each of the six prisoners in the guardhouse and question them separately. I might learn something from them."

Major Walsh shook his head. "I'm afraid that will be impossible."

Cavannagh looked surprised. "Might I ask why, sir?"

"They are no longer here. They appeared before me shortly after you and Prefontaine left to try and find that half-breed lookout. In my capacity as a justice of the peace I accepted guilty pleas from all six. I fined four of them three hundred dollars apiece as ringleaders, and the two teamsters two hundred dollars each as hirelings. Their fines were paid in full. Sixteen hundred and twenty-one dollars in all, with court costs included."

"But, sir! They didn't have enough money among them to pay one fine, let alone six."

"Their fines were paid for them."

Cavannagh took several seconds to digest that fact.

"May I ask by whom, sir?"

"You may. Mr. Michael O'Shaughnessy."

"O'Shaughnessy!"

Major Walsh seemed as surprised as Cavannagh. "You know Mr. O'Shaughnessy, Corporal?"

"No, sir. I caught him talking to the prisoners through the guardhouse window."

Major Walsh tugged at his moustache. "Hmmm. Perhaps he was deciding whether to hire them. That's why he paid their fines, although personally I think he got a bad bargain out of the deal."

"What work would he have them doing, sir?"

"He's representing a group of Winnipeg businessmen interested in opening up trading posts between there and the Rocky Mountains. At least, that's what he told me. I presume he'll employ them in some related capacity, possibly as escorts through Blackfoot country, although he doesn't really need armed escorts now that we're out here in the Territories. He could require them when he gets beyond our jurisdiction into British Columbia, however."

"He must want them pretty badly to pay money like that," Cavannagh observed wryly.

"I didn't inquire into that," Major Walsh replied gruffly. "It's perfectly legal for him to pay their fines and hire them. I have far more important matters to occupy my mind."

The thought of O'Shaughnessy rankled Cavannagh. The Irishman had told him he was going south to Fort Benton, not west across Blackfoot country to British Columbia. And there were those seven horse tracks joining the other three at the campsite down near the border. O'Shaughnessy and the six Missouri men. As well, there was the shamrock card, which Cavannagh was prepared to bet his last dollar was dropped by the red-bearded Irishman. They had all headed south for the Montana border, keeping off the regular trail, obviously because they hadn't wanted to be seen.

It all stank!

Major Walsh's voice broke into Cavannagh's thoughts.

"I'm prepared to give you the authorization you're asking, Corporal . . ." Then, catching the triumphant gleam that leaped into the younger man's eyes, the major held up his hand. "Within certain clearly understood limits."

"Yes, sir." Cavannagh couldn't conceal the eagerness in his voice.

"For the record, you're going down to Fort Benton to inquire of the I. G. Baker Company whether they've had any word of the ammunition Ottawa is sending us. But unofficially, you can take the time to

43

conduct some inquiries along the lines you've suggested. I must, however, caution you to act with the utmost discretion, Cavannagh. I don't want you doing anything foolhardy. Regardless of the fact that you're an American citizen, you're also a member of the North West Mounted Police, sworn to maintain the Queen's peace in Canadian territory, and we have to take great care not to violate any neutrality laws. The minute you learn anything of a positive nature, you're to communicate it to the United States authorities."

"I understand, sir."

The immaculate, red-coated officer pushed back his chair and stood up. Stepping around his desk, he thrust out his hand. "Good luck, Corporal."

Leaving Major Walsh's quarters, Corporal Cavannagh crossed behind the fort's open gates and entered the small Anglican Mission nursing station set against the inside palisade wall immediately south of the gates.

To his consternation, Cavannagh found Miss April Bannister packing everything into two wooden boxes.

"What are you doing?" he asked.

A beautiful, golden-haired woman in nurse's uniform looked up from the boxes. Her deep violet eyes widened with pleasure when she saw who it was.

"Hello, John. I was hoping I'd see you before I leave."

Cavannagh could hardly believe his ears. "Leave?" He glanced quickly around. "For good?"

The smile fled her face and she nodded. "Father

Dickinson has fallen ill up at Fort Edmonton and the bishop has ordered me there to take his place, at least until he's better."

Cavannagh looked like a lost dog. "I hope there's nothing seriously wrong with him."

The beautiful golden-haired woman put a hand out and touched the sleeve of his scarlet tunic. "Unfortunately he has tuberculosis."

Cavannagh's eyes sought the floor. "So you'll be gone a long time. Perhaps for good."

She nodded sadly. "I'm afraid so."

"Couldn't you refuse to go?"

"Anglican Mission nurses have to take orders, too. Just like Mounted Policemen."

"This is one Mounted Policeman who wouldn't obey an order if his heart told him not to."

"Is that why you're no longer an officer in the American army?"

She had hit a delicate spot, although unwittingly so, for he knew she would never intentionally hurt anyone. He had never told her that he had resigned his commission in the United States Army because of his involvement with a fellow officer's wife. Nor did he intend to, for he was anything but proud of it.

"It does bother you, doesn't it? I mean, not being an officer any longer?"

He took off his pillbox hat and fiddled with the narrow leather chin strap. "What bothers me right now is the thought of you going away. Especially to Fort Edmonton. It must be a thousand miles away."

"Nearer five hundred."

"It might as well be a thousand."

"Major Walsh is sending an escort with me as far as

Fort MacLeod. If you were to ask, he might let you be part of it. He likes you, you know."

Cavannagh shook his head. "I'm on the verge of leaving myself. That's why I called in now instead of this evening. I'm going almost two hundred miles in the opposite direction."

Alarm sprang into her violet eyes. "Nothing dangerous, I hope. Although where the Mounted Police are concerned, I suppose there's always an element of danger."

Cavannagh still played with his hat. "Just a ride to Fort Benton to find out where our ammunition shipment is. Nothing dangerous in that. I'll probably be back here again before you're halfway to Fort Edmonton. When do you leave?"

"Tomorrow morning."

Cavannagh looked into her eyes. Every time he did so he felt weak in the knees. He believed he was in love with her, although he had not told her. He knew she cared for him a great deal, but whether she loved him he could not tell. He was aware that she was extraordinarily dedicated to her work, and perhaps her dedication allowed no room for a man's love.

"Could I come over this evening and help you pack?"

She looked back at him and laughed sweetly. "Good gracious! I don't have that much to pack. Besides, I thought you said you were on the verge of leaving."

"I did say that, but on second thought I realize I wouldn't be that far ahead leaving this afternoon. I might as well get a good night's sleep and strike out at first light tomorrow."

She laughed again, a laugh as beautiful to listen to as she was to behold. "All right, John. I'll be delighted to have you visit me this evening."

He grinned widely. "Good. I'll be here immediately after picket."

He walked away feeling happy, although he knew he was merely delaying the inevitable pain. But he couldn't let her go away without a proper good-bye.

Chapter 4

Round, china-blue eyes gazed unblinkingly from beneath hairless eyebrows and carefully observed every detail of the small wagon train crawling across the open prairie. There were four canvas-topped wagons, each drawn by eight long-eared mules, a teamster with a long whip perched above each team. The first three wagons were covered by light gray canvas drawn taut over their metal frames. But the fourth was startlingly different—its canvas was an outlandish orange, made even brighter by its newness.

"Hell!" a voice croaked from behind the watcher's ear. "On'y ten blue-bellies. This'll be plumb easy, Egg-Head."

"Shut up!" Egg-Head snapped over his shoulder. "Eyes I got."

Ten blue-shirted cavalrymen rode in pairs stretched along the length of the small train. Snatches of conversation drifted above the rumble of the wagons and the curses of the mule skinners, carried up to the ridge where Egg-Head and his gang looked down on the sun-bleached Montana trail stretching west toward the Bear Paws between the Milk to the north and the Missouri to the south. One of the soldiers was an officer—even at this distance Egg-Head could see the broad yellow stripe down his pants. Probably a lieutenant. The one riding next to him would be a sergeant, and the other eight, troopers.

Egg-Head had twenty men, not one under thirty-three years of age, all seasoned fighters, veterans of the Civil War. Ruthless men unsuited by temperament for a life other than one of violence. Dangerous men who had been unable to adjust to the absence of action once the war was over. Wild men unwilling to buckle down to the discipline of a postwar, Indian-fighting army that would have not only satisfied their lust for excitement but welcomed them as well. It took a strong man to control them. Egg-Head Vinsett, a buckskin-clad monster of a man hulking three hundred and fifty pounds of bulk and towering six feet six inches high, possessed the strength.

Not only the strength but the ferocity as well. For Egg-Head was a fighter whose savagery could match the cruelest Indian on the plains, evidenced by the notched Sioux scalping knife he wore on his belt.

"How're we goin' to take 'em, Egg-Head?" asked one of the men kneeling on the ridge with him. Strangely enough, Egg-Head Vinsett didn't mind his nickname. None of his men had ever heard his first name, and it had been so long since he'd heard it himself, he'd almost forgotten it. And *Egg-Head* described him well, for that was exactly how his head looked. Set smack on his shoulders with no neck at all, his head was round and smooth, completely hairless. In fact, Egg-Head's entire body was as smooth as his face, without a hair on it.

"We're goin' to head down back of this ridge, swing around to the west, an' cut into 'em when they go to cross that dry streambed yonder," Egg-Head answered.

"That don't give us no cover," commented another man.

Egg-Head turned and focused his round china-blue eyes on the man who had just spoken.

"What the hell you want cover for, Cousins? You runnin' scared?"

Nervously rubbing the palm of his hand down the side of his pants, Cousins watched the sun glint off a small gold ring hanging from Egg-Head's left ear-lobe.

"I ain't runnin' scared."

"Then shut yo' goddamn mouth."

Egg-Head scrambled to his feet, moved down the sloping back of the ridge with amazing speed and agility for such a colossus, reached the horses, and hurled his immense mass into the saddle with a force that nearly brought his coal-black seventeen-hander to its knees.

Impatiently grabbing up the reins, Egg-Head dug his spurs into the black horse's flanks and bellowed: "Move out, goddamn it. Bluecoats we kill."

Twenty-one horses drummed over the dry, dusty ground at the base of the ridge. It took them fifteen minutes to clear the ridge's extremity. The riders couldn't see the army mule train because it had dipped below a rise in the prairie, but they followed Egg-Head's gigantic, buckskin-covered figure.

The mule train was struggling across the rock-filled bottom of the dry streambed when Egg-Head's raiders struck. Because the iron-rimmed wagon wheels made such a ringing clatter on the smooth, round rocks, the soldiers didn't hear the hoofbeats until it was too late. By that time the attackers were almost on them.

There was no real strategy behind the attack. It was simply a wide open, hell-bent-for-leather charge, a wild guerrilla-type strike that had served many of them so well during the war. They spread out in a long, sweeping single line, each presenting as difficult a target as possible, firing as they rode.

The first the escorting cavalrymen knew of the attack was when the vicious rolling boom of a .45 caliber Sharps buffalo rifle cut through the customary sounds of the mule train—iron on rock, creaking wagon springs, snorting horses, cussing teamsters—and the lieutenant pitched from his saddle. Almost immediately a second bluecoat toppled.

Panic seized the soldiers until their sergeant got a grip on them and cursed them into defensive positions away from the wagons, opening fire on the spread-out line of charging riders.

But the soldiers didn't stand a chance. Although their sergeant coolly directed a return fire, six of the remaining eight cavalrymen were little better than raw recruits, and their single-shot Springfields against Winchester repeaters in seasoned hands further stacked the odds against them. When a second shot from Egg-Head's deadly buffalo rifle blew the top off the sergeant's head, the remaining soldiers were ready to drop their carbines and throw up their hands. They never got the chance — Egg-Head's raiders relentlessly gunned down the green young men.

"Kill 'em all, goddamn it," bellowed Egg-Head. "No goddamn survivors! Them mule skinners, too, goddamn it!"

A mule skinner's whip cracked out and twirled its snakelike end around a raider's throat. The raider screamed in pain for a second until the noise gurgled out. Egg-Head's .45 Sharps exploded at close range and the teamster was blown apart.

A second teamster threw down his whip. "The army hired me t' skin mules, not fight."

But Egg-Head blew him apart, and the third as well. The fourth, stark terror stamped on his face, turned and ran blindly up the rocky bed, not having any idea where he was going, just desperate to escape the carnage. Egg-Head blew a gaping, ragged hole in his back.

"Hell, Egg-Head. You shouldna' ought to have killed all them skinners. Now we ain't got none to drive them teams."

Egg-Head was lowering his smoking buffalo gun when the raider called Cousins spoke those words from just off to his right. In a sudden blur of movement, Egg-Head whirled around and crashed the heavy, long-barreled rifle across Cousins's face, knocking him backward head over heels from his saddle. The next instant Egg-Head heaved his three hundred and fifty pounds of bone, fat, and muscle from his horse's back to land almost on top of the raider. With his right hand Egg-Head grabbed Cousins by the hair and jerked his head up, then with his left he drew the wicked-looking broad-bladed Sioux scalping knife from a beaded buckskin sheath on a wide studded leather belt holding in his great bulging belly, and held the razor-sharp blade so tight against Cousins's forehead just below the hairline that it drew blood.

Cousins screamed!

The other raiders, startled, looked over.

"The mouth you got is gonna get you into trouble, you goddamn ass-burnin' son of a bitch!"

Beads of sweat popped out on Cousins's forehead, mixing with the red blood that began to wash down to his wide, rolling, terror-stricken eyes. He couldn't move, couldn't even struggle, because Egg-Head's knee pressed into his stomach and he held the head up so rigidly by the hair, the scalping knife still sharply in place, that any movement Cousins made would result in a further loss of his scalp.

"The only thing savin' your useless goddamn hide is the Colonel wantin' every gun we got, even one that don't shoot straight. Otherwise I'd lift your mangy scalp an' leave you out here for the prairie wolves."

Egg-Head released his grip, crawled off the terrified Cousins, and wiped his bloody knife on his buckskin trousers. Shoving the knife back in its sheath, he glowered down on the blood-covered face.

"One more time you open your goddamn mouth, I'm gonna stuff your scalp in it."

Egg-Head picked up his buffalo gun and waddled over the rocky streambed to the orange-covered wagon. Only fleetingly he looked at the black lettering stenciled on the bright canvas—*U.S. Army Ord-nance*. He couldn't read, but he knew what it meant. Impatiently untying the lashings, he pulled aside one of the flaps and peered inside the hot, stuffy interior. A grin of satisfaction twisted his rounded face. He pulled the flap back into place and retied the lash-ings. Then he ambled over to each of the three canvas-covered wagons and looked in. They were not lashed, their back flaps blowing free in the wind, the front ones pulled wide open. They contained heavy wooden crates of ammunition, a few kegs of gunpow-der, and some miscellaneous military stores.

When Egg-Head finished looking into the last one, his raiders sat their saddles in a long line facing the four wagons. The war was ten years behind them— none of them had been on an army payroll since then, and more than half had ridden in irregular guerrilla outfits—but collectively they still bore a military sort of stamp. There were only eighteen of them now. The lifeless sergeant had killed two of them before Egg-Head's deadly accurate Sharps fin-ished his army service. Their bodies lay limply over their saddles. Egg-Head's raiders never left behind the bodies of their own men—only those of their victims.

Egg-Head planted his beefy legs wide apart, leaned the Sharps against his bulging belly, and hooked his thick thumbs into his broad studded leather belt. He ran his china-blue eyes along the length of them as he spoke.

"We gonna fox the army into thinkin' the Sioux got these wagons. So while you boys hurry up and git 'em movin', I'm gonna scalp each one of these blue-bellies. This is one supply train we don't want the army gettin' any idea where it's gone."

A gray-whiskered scarecrow of a man, older than the others, cackled. "That's right, Egg-Head. We'll whisk these wagons up north 'cross the border into the Cypress Hills. Then we'll give them mounted redcoats a hell of a surprise that'll blow 'em to Kingdom Come."

Egg-Head leered back. "That's right, Loon-Bin. Now get 'em rolling to hell out of here before an army patrol happens along."

The raiders legged their horses into action. Five or six of them grabbed the mule teams' traces and tried to jerk and pull the balky long-eared animals into movement. When that didn't work, they mixed their efforts with good strong cuss words. When that combination also failed to bring about the desired results, Egg-Head picked up one of the mule skinners' whips and cracked it over the long ears of the team pulling the last wagon, the one with the orange cover. The startled animals leaped forward suddenly, almost clambering into the back of the wagon immediately ahead. Then two or three of the raiders picked up the other whips and did the same, and the wagons rumbled and bounced out of the rock-filled bed and slowly climbed the shallow rise back onto the prairie.

Egg-Head glanced very briefly at the ten blue-uniformed bodies spread out on the rocky brown ground around him. His china-blue eyes rested momentarily on the yellow-striped sergeant, the top of his head blown off, lying white-faced in a drained pool of red blood. A touch of regret swept over Egg-Head's face, not for the sergeant's death, but because this was a scalp denied him.

"Shoulda shot him in the belly," Egg-Head mused to himself. "Cheatin' son of a bitch!"

Then he stepped over to the lieutenant's body. The officer's blue cavalry hat had come partway off his head. Egg-Head kicked it away, knelt down, twisted his right hand around the lieutenant's hair, and with his left hand reached for the Sioux scalping knife at his belt.

Chapter 5

Cavannagh sauntered along the board sidewalk of Fort Benton's dusty main street, glancing over at the three stern-wheelers docked at the wooden wharves facing the trading stores, saloons, gambling dens, music halls, greasy restaurants, bawdy houses, and a variety of unpainted ramshackle structures of differing shapes and sizes. He paused. River steamers had always fascinated him.

He could read the names on large oblong plates fastened to the wheelhouses or the upper-deck railings. On the first, *Rosebud*, Negro deckhands padded on calloused bare feet down a long wooden gangway. Bales of buffalo skins were piled on the wharf beside her, ready to be loaded aboard for shipment to the East. *Mirrabelle II* was the second vessel. Nothing was going on around her, but the third, *River Mermaid*, was bustling with activity. Smoke spiraled thinly skyward from her tall black funnel, while a long line of passengers threaded down the gangway from the main deck to the wharf. Mostly men — trappers and miners in rough frontier clothing, a couple of well-dressed dandies whom Cavannagh guessed were gamblers, then three overpainted and overdressed women who looked like prostitutes from the bawdy houses.

But it was a party of a dozen or more soldiers filing down the gangway that held Cavannagh's attention, and he felt a pang of yearning shoot through him as he remembered the exhilarating sensation of commanding half a troop of cavalry, the rattle of sabre scabbards, the jingle of harness, the smell of saddle soap, the stirring strains of "Garry Owen." With the realization that he no longer belonged, the pang sharpened. Then he shook the feeling and viewed them more dispassionately. They were infantry, not elite cavalrymen like the Seventh, and they looked young, little more than recruits. The lieutenant in charge couldn't have been out of the Point much more than six months. They were probably reinforcements for Fort Benton's small military detachment. Benton had never been a regular military station; it owed the designation *fort* to the old American Fur Company when it had been the principal fur trading post on the upper Missouri some twenty-five years earlier. All that remained of the old fort were a few rotting logs of the old stockade.

Spurs jingling on the sidewalk, Cavannagh resumed his saunter. He fitted in with the local inhabitants, mostly transients — buffalo hunters, cowpunchers, river men, drifters, long-bearded mountain men, a few desperadoes. His black boots, blue cavalry pants from which he'd cut the wide yellow stripes, fringed buckskin jacket, and dark blue cavalry hat made him look like an ex-soldier. There were enough around, but the unemployed ones were able to find jobs readily enough if they wanted to by signing back on with the army now that trouble was building with the Sioux and Cheyenne.

When he reached a large, freshly white-painted front, he turned in and pushed through the door to find himself inside the I. G. Baker Company trading store. A clerk led him to a spacious office at the rear of the building where Cavannagh introduced himself to Mr. Culver, the assistant manager, a tall, thin man wearing a green eyeshade.

"You don't look like a Canadian Mounted Policeman," Mr. Culver said, rising from behind a large mahogany desk.

Cavannagh grinned. "How is a Canadian Mounted Policeman supposed to look in Montana, Mr. Culver?"

The serious-faced Culver shook his head. "I hadn't thought about that. I don't suppose he'd be wearing a red coat. But you look more like one of our soldiers."

"I used to be before I went up to Canada and joined the Mounted Police."

"Oh! I would have thought all the Mounted Police were Canadians or British. Not Americans."

"I was born in Canada but I grew up in the United States." Then Cavannagh asked about the ammunition shipment.

"It looks like you've had a wasted trip," Culver replied. "Just yesterday I sent a messenger to Major

59

Walsh informing him that the ammunition has arrived at Bismark. It'll be shipped from there by riverboat, and when it gets here we'll freight it to Fort Walsh by bull train."

Cavannagh pushed his hat back off his forehead. "My trip hasn't been wasted. I've something else to do while I'm here."

"I see." Culver rubbed his hands together. "Well, if there's anything I can help you with . . ."

"There is." Cavannagh tapped his black cavalry belt, with its awkward, wrist-twisting closed holster. "I'd like a gun belt a little more practical than this."

When he left the store ten minutes later, Cavannagh wore his Smith & Wesson .44 in a stiff, brand-new open holster on his right hip, attached to a bullet-looped gun belt equally stiff. Its newness felt clumsily strange and he felt conspicuous wearing it. However, he put that feeling aside to concentrate on finding Dutch Schultz.

He didn't know any of Dutch Schultz's hangouts, but he reckoned the saloons were good places to start. Pushing through the swing doors of the first one he came to, he made his way through the unaccustomed dimness to the bar and ordered a whisky. When his eyes adjusted to the light he looked around. The place was half full—men sitting at tables, a few standing at the bar. Typical types to be found on the Missouri plains. Most were talking in twos or threes, a few playing cards, two or three observing him, not with hostility but with the simple curiosity they attached to a stranger. As soon as someone else entered, they'd swing their eyes to him.

Dutch Schultz certainly wasn't in the place. Nor did the bartender know of him.

Cavannagh downed his drink, left the saloon, and went into the next. This time he was joined by a brightly painted strawberry-blond dancing girl.

"Like to buy a gal a drink, tall-dark-and-handsome?" she asked seductively.

Cavannagh wasn't in the mood for women, particularly not blonds, not even strawberry-blonds. April Bannister was very much on his mind. When they had said good-bye that night at Fort Walsh, Cavannagh had left with the impression that he was more upset over their parting than she was. He had consoled himself by reasoning that her dedication to her work came first in her life. Perhaps she was stronger than him. Or perhaps she didn't love him but simply regarded him as a good friend. Anyway, he had mooned over her during the four-day ride to Fort Benton. Damn women! Why did he have to fall in love with them?

To the bartender he said, "Give the lady whatever she wants, and I'll have a whisky."

When the bartender served his drink, Cavannagh asked him whether he knew Dutch Schultz. Upon receiving a negative answer, he downed his whisky, nodded to the dancing girl, and turned to go.

"Hey, where are you goin', handsome?" The dancing girl's voice was full of surprise.

The moment he was outside on Front Street, he made up his mind to ask Major Walsh for a transfer to Fort Saskatchewan, only twenty miles from Fort Edmonton, as soon as he got back to the Cypress

Hills post.

At the third saloon, his mention of Dutch Schultz's name brought a momentary hesitation and a hardening glint in the bartender's eye.

"Nope! Never heard of him."

Cavannagh knew it was a lie. This wasn't the ex-cavalry officer's first time in Benton and he knew this particular saloon was a notorious hangout for Missouri badmen.

"That's odd," Cavannagh said, toying with his still-full whisky glass. "He used to come in here a lot."

The big, gruff bartender said, "Lots o' men come in here, soldier-boy. I don't bother askin' names."

"You should. You might find yourself serving a drink to President Grant himself." With that, Cavannagh tipped his untouched glass upside down on top of the bar, the amber fluid slopping along the polished top.

"What the hell—!" the bartender exploded. But Cavannagh had turned around and went striding out of the saloon.

He made his way to a blacksmith's shop where he had left his horse to have a pulled shoe replaced. He had decided to spend the night in Benton, so from the smith's he took his horse to a nearby livery stable. He was about to leave the livery stable, his saddlebags over his shoulder and a Winchester in his hand, when a flint-hard voice crackled from behind him.

"How is it you're lookin' for Dutch Schultz, soldierboy?"

Cavannagh turned around slowly, to find himself looking into black crowlike eyes set well back in a long, thin face completely devoid of any expression. The face was clean-shaven but the beginning of a heavy whisker stubble covered his jaw. His cheeks were flat and his skin was drawn so tight across the bone structure that it looked as though any movement would crack it. Only the glittering eyes seemed alive. On his head he wore a high-crowned cowboy hat. Around his waist hung a low-slung Colt, its butt jutting out at an ominous angle. The inside of the holster bore a thin shaft of smooth, oiled metal to allow for a faster draw, and the bottom was tied to the man's leg. A gunslinger!

"Do you know where I can find him?" Cavannagh asked.

Without moving his mouth, the gunslinger replied, "I'm askin' the questions, soldier-boy."

Cavannagh let his saddlebags slide off his shoulder. They landed with a distinct slapping noise on the straw-covered floor. "Then I'd advise you to mind your own business."

The gunslinger flicked his crow eyes to the .44 on Cavannagh's hip. "If you want to go on seein' the sun come up, you'd better be as handy with that shootin' iron as you are with your mouth."

Cavannagh caught his meaning. "I'm no quick-draw man."

"Then you shouldn't be wearin' an iron."

Cavannagh looked steadily back into the gunslinger's beadlike eyes. The Winchester in his right hand, he slowly moved his left to the buckle of his gun belt and unbuckled the stiff leather. The belt fell to the floor. "Now I'm not wearing one."

63

A grin cracked the gunslinger's tight face. "Yaller, huh?"

Cavannagh shook his head. "I don't like your odds. But perhaps you'll like mine." He lifted up his Winchester and levered all but one of the bullets out through the ejection slot. "I'll take this Winchester across to the other side of the street out there . . . that'll be about fifty, sixty yards. Then I'll match you . . . the one bullet in this Winchester against the six in your six-shooter. That sound fair?"

The gunslinger wasn't grinning anymore. "Are you tryin' to be funny?"

"Does a .44-40 right between your eyes sound like a laughing matter?"

The gunslinger stood staring at Cavannagh. After several seconds a muscle in the gunslinger's left cheek quivered, pulling the skin down below his eye. Cavannagh tried to keep a triumphant gleam from showing in his eyes.

Finally the gunslinger said, "I'll give you until you get to the other side of the street."

They both turned to go, but suddenly the gunslinger reached for his six-shooter, crouched, and whirled. But Cavannagh anticipated the move, spun around at the same time, and swept his Winchester up barrel-first to catch the gunslinger a cracking blow across his face. The gunslinger's Colt cleared leather, crashed thunderously, and a bullet zipped past Cavannagh's shoulder. Cavannagh brought the rifle back, hitting the gunslinger on the side of the head and knocking him flying. Before the gunslinger could get to his feet again, the ex-cavalry officer drove the

Winchester butt into the back of his neck, flattening him facedown on the floor.

Cavannagh knelt down, picked up the .44-40 cartridges from the floor, and fed them back into his Winchester. He was buckling his gun belt back on when another voice called from behind him.

"Hold it!"

Once more Cavannagh turned. In the stable doorway stood a tall middle-aged man with the typical heavy moustache of the period and a dull silver star on his vest. A blue-metaled six-gun was held in his hand. He looked at Cavannagh, then at the gunslinger's prone body.

"What's goin' on in here?"

Cavannagh didn't reply immediately, preferring to let the peace officer deduce the answer from his own observation. But the deduction wasn't what Cavannagh expected.

"You better hand me your guns. I'm arrestin' you for assault."

"Assault! You've got it all mixed up, Sheriff."

The peace officer fixed the younger man with a jaundiced eye. "Watch your words, young fella. I take it the way I sees it, and right now I sees him lyin' there on the floor and you standin' above him. The way I sees it, he didn't assault you none."

The sound of the shot had attracted a few onlookers, one of whom was the livery keeper. A touch of gunpowder lingered faintly in the air and the livery keeper noticed a couple of the horses still nervously stamping in their stalls and bunched up close to the walls, heads turning apprehensively around, watching these strange-yet-familiar two-legged creatures. The noise of the Colt had been near-deafening in the confines of the stables. Angered, the livery keeper stomped right up to the sheriff and pointed down at the prone gunslinger.

"One thing, Sheriff — he ain't got no business in my stables. He ain't got no horse in hyar an' ah don't appreciate none him lettin' off his shootin' iron in hyar."

"How d' you know it was him what fired that shot?"

The livery keeper pointed again. "Pretty obvious, ain't it? That's gotta be his gun there on the floor."

The Colt had slithered across the floor to stop half-hidden among some straw. The sheriff hesitated.

"That's the man you should be arresting, Sheriff," Cavannagh said. "Attempted murder. He was trying to kill me. That's why I hit him. Look at his holster."

"That's right, Sheriff," interjected the livery keeper. "Look at that holster. Tied down and all — "

"Shut up!" the sheriff rasped impatiently. "I'm the goddamn sheriff around here."

The sheriff craned his neck for a better look, and as understanding slowly crossed his face he shoved his pistol back into its holster.

"How bad's he hurt?"

"He'll have a headache when he wakes up," Cavannagh said.

The peace officer nodded at a couple of the onlookers. "Load him onto a wagon and bring him over to the jail. I'll lock him up. You" — he indicated Cavannagh — "can come and help me write up what happened."

At the sheriff's office Cavannagh signed a few awkwardly written lines of statement. When the sheriff asked him what his business was in Benton, Cavannagh was cautiously evasive, bearing in mind Major Walsh's instructions to act with the utmost discretion. Were the man a United States marshal, Cavannagh would have been a fraction more revealing, but Benton peace officers had occasionally borne less than savory reputations. However, talking with this one, Cavannagh formed the opinion that he was straight enough if a trifle slow.

"Have you heard of Dutch Schultz?"

"Dutch Schultz? Yeah. Friend of yours?"

"Not exactly, but I'm looking for him."

"So are a few others. He got on the wrong side of the wrong people, and there's supposed to be some guns out lookin' for him." He jerked his thumb over his shoulder in the direction of the cells, where the gunslinger was sitting nursing a damned sore neck and a cracking headache. "Maybe he's one of them."

Cavannagh realized the sheriff wasn't so slow after all. "You wouldn't know where I might find him?"

The sheriff shook his head. "Heard he's holed up in the hills west of here, but that could mean covering a hell of a lot of ground. I guess that's why he's still alive—if they haven't got to him yet."

"Hmmm. Well, if you don't require anything further of me, Sheriff, I'll be on my way."

"All right."

Cavannagh picked up his Winchester and saddlebags and headed toward the door.

"You keep out of trouble now, young fella."

Cavannagh waved the Winchester in reply, opened the door, and stepped out. His boots had barely hit the board sidewalk when he glanced up the wide street to see three horsemen riding out of town. One of them was a half-breed wearing a tall black stovepipe hat!

Chapter 6

Fort Benton was five hours behind them and the sun was reddening the vast open sky ahead when the three horsemen sighted the low, unpainted buildings of a small ranch spread out below an upflung mass of rock that formed the immediate horizon.

They didn't speak, just sat their rocking saddles and watched the ranch buildings get closer. It wasn't much of a ranch — really no more than a homestead with a house only big enough to accommodate a small family, a modest barn, a storeroom, a corral, a water well. The sound of their horses' hoofs on the hard autumn-browned, grass-covered earth had announced their approach, for a man and a young freckle-faced boy appeared in the doorway.

The man was balding and bearded. Although he was no more than forty, years of toil had lined his face to a weathered sixty. Not a big man, no more than five eight, but solid, he wore no shirt, just a sweat-stained woolen undershirt with the top two buttons missing, revealing tufts of chest hair poking out through the opening. His smoke-blackened trousers were held up by both a belt and a pair of wide leather suspenders, and cracked, dust-caked boots covered his feet.

As the three horsemen reined to in front of a slightly sagging veranda, the man put his arm around the boy's shoulder and nodded.

"Howdy."

One of the men nodded back. "Howdy."

The other man and the half-breed under the tall black stovepipe hat said nothing, just sat their saddles and looked stonily at the man and the boy. The bearded homesteader didn't like their looks. He had seen a lot of trouble in his life and he recognized it now. Instinctively, protectively, he drew the boy closer to him.

"Anything I can do for you fellas?" Apprehension shaded his voice.

"We wanna look around," said the one who had already spoken. As he eased himself forward in his saddle and swung his right leg over his horse's back to dismount, the other man and the half-breed snaked Winchesters out of saddle scabbards.

Stark concern cracked the homesteader's voice. "Hey — what is this?"

The first man climbed the veranda step and pushed the homesteader and the boy aside. The homesteader's arm shot out to grab at his back but the metallic snick-snick of Winchester levers stopped him.

"Yew jes' stand right where yew are, cow chip," grated the second horseman, his rifle pointed at the homesteader's stomach, "an' yew mightn't git hurt."

Then he spoke out of the side of his mouth to the half-breed. "Look around out back at them buildin's, Buffalo Johnny."

Without a word of acknowledgment, not even a

70

grunt, the half-breed flicked his horse's reins and, Winchester pointed to the sky, rode around to the unpainted, crudely built structures at the back.

Inside the house the first man looked around the kitchen. A frightened woman clutching a faded gingham apron stood by a burning black wood stove.

The man tipped his hat with his left hand and nodded. "Ma'am." His right hand hovered over his gun butt.

He paid her no further attention and went on into the bedrooms. He peered out the windows, and saw the half-breed riding toward the barn.

The woman still stood by the stove when the spur-clinking intruder walked back into the kitchen. Transfixed, her eyes clung to him, watching his every move. He nodded to her again and stepped back outside.

"Your name is Moore, ain't it?" he asked the homesteader.

The homesteader nodded quickly. "That's right."

"Hear tell you're a friend of Dutch Schultz."

The homesteader's eyes darted from the one man's face to the other, understanding in his eyes. The man grinned. "Also hear tell you're hidin' him around here somewheres."

The homesteader's lips dried.

"All you gotta do is tell us where he's at."

The homesteader licked his lips.

"You ain't much of a talker, are you?" the first man said. But he said no more, simply standing on the veranda with the homesteader and his son. The second man sat his saddle silently, his rifle still pointing at the homesteader.

Then Buffalo Johnny rode around the corner of

the house, his dark face expressionless, his rifle butt resting on his thigh, barrel pointed to the sky. He stopped beside the second man.

The first man looked up at him. The half-breed shook his head. The first man turned again to the homesteader.

"Schultz ain't on your property. Leastwise, not right around here, he ain't. Where is he?"

The homesteader shook his head. "I don't know any Dutch Schultz."

The first man suddenly brought his arm up and savagely backhanded the homesteader, snapping his head sideways and drawing a gush of blood to his mouth.

"Don't lie to me, damn you!"

The boy lunged at the man, his straight-out arms jabbing the man in the stomach, catching him by surprise and sending him reeling.

"Leave my dad alone!" the boy screamed.

"You little—"

The second horseman's Winchester exploded, the horse jerking its head at the unexpected thunderously sharp noise immediately behind its ear. The bullet sped between the boy and his father, thudding into the wooden wall. The woman inside the house came screaming to the door just as the first man recovered his balance, grabbed the boy, and roughly heaved him down off the veranda to the hard ground below.

The homesteader jumped onto his son's assailant.

"Goddamn you—" the first man snarled, grabbing at the homesteader.

The second man levered his Winchester again and pointed it at the fighting homesteader, but he didn't fire for fear of hitting his companion. The two combatants fell heavily to the ground below the veranda, rolling around at the feet of the nervously snorting horses as they pranced back out of the way. The woman stood helplessly screaming in the doorway, her hands holding her head.

"Shut up!" the second horseman shouted, waving his rifle at her. "Shut up an' git back inside."

"Git off'n that damned horse an' git this son of a bitch off'n me, Jiggs," panted the first man, fighting to get from under the angered homesteader.

The horseman called Jiggs sat his saddle, confused, pointing his rifle down at the two struggling figures.

The maddened homesteader had both his hands around the horseman's throat, choking the life out of him. The gagging horseman's face went purple, his hands clutching at the homesteader's ironlike wrists.

"*Jiggs!* Git him off'n—" His further words were drowned in a flood of his own vomit.

But it was Buffalo Johnny who acted. He swung his horse around in front of the confused Jiggs, pushing Jiggs's horse out of the way until he was over the two struggling figures. Then he sharply swept his Winchester barrel across the homesteader's ear. The homesteader's grasp around the horseman's throat weakened. Buffalo Johnny hit him again. The homesteader slumped. Weakly, the gasping horseman rolled the homesteader's body off him and struggled slowly to his knees and rested.

Concern covered Jiggs's face as he looked down at his heaving companion. "You all right, Clay?"

Clay rubbed his fingers along his burning neck. For

73

more than a minute he didn't answer, and when he did the words wheezed out of his mouth. "That mother-lovin' son of a bitch . . . I'm gonna kill 'im."

The boy had got up and run crying to his father when his mother almost immediately joined him. Buffalo Johnny sat motionless in his saddle, his dark face devoid of any expression.

When Clay recovered sufficiently to get to his feet, the bearded homesteader had regained consciousness and, aided by his wife and son, pulled himself to a sitting position. Clay stepped over and stood glaring down at him.

"You're gonna pay for that, Moore," he croaked, still rubbing his throat with one hand while the other rested threateningly on his gun handle.

"Why don't you just git an' leave us alone?" the woman shouted.

"You better git back inside where you belong, woman," Clay wheezed.

But the woman held her ground.

"I don't usually git rough with women, but if'n I have to, I sure will. Now do as you're told."

"No! Leave us alone!"

Clay grabbed her by the arm and dragged her up the steps. Moore, the homesteader, tried to get to his feet, but Clay lashed out with his boot, caught him under the chin, and sent him toppling backward. The boy jumped up at his father's attacker, but Clay's free hand grasped the boy's straw-colored hair. He dragged them both inside the house, heaved them across the floor, and slammed the door shut on them. Then he hurled himself off the veranda onto the homesteader, grabbed him by the neck of his woolen

74

undershirt, and yanked him to his feet. The next instant he slammed him against the veranda post with near-back-breaking force.

"Now you tell me where Dutch Schultz is, you miserable son of a bitch, or I'm gonna blow a forty-five right up your nose."

Emphasizing his words, Clay drew his pistol and shoved the cold metal barrel end against the homesteader's nose.

"If I tell you, how do I know you won't kill me, anyways?" the homesteader managed to ask.

Clay thought about that for a moment, reasoning overcoming his anger. He needed to find out where Schultz was. After that, he could deal with this rotten bastard. Christ, he'd nearly caved in his windpipe.

Clay holstered his pistol, released his grip on the homesteader, and stepped back. "All we want is Dutch Schultz. We ain't got no argument with you, Moore. Tell us where Schultz is an' we ride away."

Momentarily freed, the homesteader held his aching jaw and stared at the ground as though in thought.

"But don't spend too long thinkin' 'bout it," the horseman called Clay prodded. "You ain't got no choice. You either tell us damned swift-like, or we're gonna burn this place of your'n to the ground an' you an' your woman an' kid with it."

Fear leaped into the homesteader's eyes!

Just at that moment the house door flew open and the homesteader's wife stood framed in the doorway. In her hands she held a well-used single-shot Springfield rifle pointed squarely at Clay. Clay went for his pistol as he swung around to face her, but the homesteader desperately struck out with his dirt-caked boot and caught Clay full in the testicles, doubling him up. The Springfield went off and the bullet tore through the top of his hat and bored straight on through the center of his down-plunging head.

Jiggs's startled horse shied sideways and Jiggs's Winchester went off, the bullet thudding harmlessly into the door frame. Jiggs cursed and fought to bring his horse under control, but suddenly his eyes bulged, his face froze into an expression of amazement, and he pitched forward out of his saddle. A moment later a rifle explosion boomed across the open space from somewhere well behind him.

Before anything else could happen, a shrill, high-pitched yell pierced the air and the half-breed galloped furiously away, his legs thumping his horse's sides, his body flattened low over the animal's back. A second bullet from the hidden rifle followed him, spinning the tall black hat from his head, but the half-breed disappeared behind the buildings, reappearing seconds later on the far side, zigzagging his horse's flight and sliding over its off side Indian-style as he galloped on.

The homesteader and his wife turned their eyes in the direction from where the rifle shots had come. They saw riding toward them a lone horseman, a rifle held across his saddle. He had to be a friend, but just in case . . .

"Hand me ol' Betsy, Martha . . . and hurry inside and rustle up some bullets."

The lone horseman rode closer. The homesteader watched him. He couldn't recognize him, didn't know who he might be, but there was something about him that comforted the homesteader. He sat tall and straight in the saddle, sat his saddle like a soldier, and as he got closer still, Moore could recognize army clothing—the hat, trousers, boots. But no badges . . . and a buckskin jacket. So he wasn't army now. Maybe a peace officer. Soon the horseman was close enough that the homesteader could see his face—there was something about him . . .

"Good day," Cavannagh said, nodding to the homesteader and touching his hat brim to the homesteader's wife, who had returned to her husband's side. "Looks like you've had some trouble."

The homesteader put down his Springfield. "Not no more . . . thanks to you."

Cavannagh glanced off in the direction where the half-breed had finally disappeared at the far end of the rock mass stretching above and beyond the ranch. Dust from his passing still drifted above the ground. The ex-cavalry officer slid his Winchester back into its saddle bucket, climbed down off the horse, and examined the two dead men.

"You a law officer, mister?" the homesteader asked, looking down at Cavannagh as he studied the faces and went through their pockets. It was a fair question, for Cavannagh had an air of authority.

"In a manner of speaking," Cavannagh answered. "I'm working in conjunction with the government. Do you know either one of these men?"

The homesteader shook his head. "No. Never seen 'em before."

There was nothing in Clay's pockets of any consequence, certainly nothing that told Cavannagh any-

77

thing he wanted to know. Jiggs's body was still twitching and it took some effort on Cavannagh's part to search him. When he had finished, he stood up.

"Why were they bothering you?" When the homesteader didn't answer, Cavannagh asked further, "Were they looking for Dutch Schultz?"

It had been little more than a stab in the dark, but the homesteader's face told Cavannagh that he was on the right track. Sighing wearily, the man sat down slowly on the veranda step. "So you're lookin' for him, too."

"Yes, but not to do him any harm. We rode together a bit up in Canada."

The homesteader looked at Cavannagh with renewed interest. "Say—you wouldn't be—what's your name, mister?"

"Cavannagh."

The homesteader grinned. "You're the ex-cavalry lieutenant that went up to Canada and joined that new mounted police outfit they got up there. Dutch told me about you." The grin left his face. "You're not fixin' to take him back to Canada, are you?"

"No. I need his help. He might be able to give me some information."

The homesteader got up from the step. Once more concern showed on his face. "How did you know to come to me lookin' for Dutch? He wouldn't have told you."

Cavannagh pointed at the two dead men. "I saw them in Benton with that half-breed and followed them here. I was after that half-breed in Canada."

The sun had gone down behind the rocks and the

sky was darkening quickly.

"I guess I'd better bury 'em," the homesteader said. "I don't feel like haulin' 'em into Benton."

"I'll help you."

"Obliged. Martha was gettin' the supper on when they come along. It might've suffered a bit by the waitin', but I reckon she can right it. We'd feel plumb good t' have you join us."

Cavannagh smiled. "Thank you. I'd appreciate that. It's been a long time since I ate a home-cooked meal."

Chapter 7

Using the long blue line of mountains to the west as a landmark, Cavannagh rode southwestward over rolling grassland. The golden ball of morning sun was slanting down over his left shoulder when he topped a hill and saw a line shack over just short of another rise. Without a pause he legged his big bay gelding ahead. He was halfway there, completely exposed in the open, when a bullet whip-cracked over his head, almost immediately followed by the echoing crack-roll of a Winchester.

Cupping his hands to his mouth, Cavannagh shouted. "Hold your fire, Dutch. It's Cavannagh."

"What the hell are you doin' back in Montana?" a voice shouted from the shack. "You desert the Mounted Police?"

"I'm looking for you," Cavannagh yelled in reply.

"With or without an extradition warrant?"

"Without. Let me come on."

"Anyone back there over that hill behind you?"

"No."

"Okay. Come on."

When he was about a dozen yards from the shack, the door opened and Dutch Schultz, rifle in hand, stood back almost obscured in the dimness.

"Put your horse in the corral and come inside."

A big roan stood in the corral behind the shack. Cavannagh unsaddled his bay, took off the bridle, and stepped around to the open door carrying his Winchester. Schultz moved aside to let him in, then put down his rifle, and seated himself on a rickety chair beside a food-littered table.

Not two months had passed since Cavannagh last saw Dutch Schultz, yet he was shocked at the change in him. He had lost weight and the quick grin and the mocking humor in the pale blue eyes were gone, replaced instead by a furtive, hunted look. He wore a beard now, matted and food stained, and his blond hair was lank and greasy. He was older than Cavannagh by a good ten years, having fought all through the war, and he looked every day of it. Strapped around his waist were two six-guns, and a second Winchester stood in a corner. Two boxes of shells were on the dirt floor beside the bunk he slept in.

"You're all set to stand off a small army," Cavannagh observed.

"And to ride the hell outta here when I run short of bullets," Schultz added, inclining his head to a saddle and bedroll covering a bunk on the other side of the shack.

"Who's after you, Dutch?"

Schultz shook his head. "You wouldn't know them." Then, in a different tone, "How the hell did you find me, anyways?"

"Buffalo Johnny . . . I saw him in Benton with two other fellows and followed them to Moore's homestead. They were trying to make him tell them were you were when I came along."

"Buffalo Johnny! That son of a bitch! Where the hell are they now?"

Cavannagh told him what happened. Schultz scowled.

"If I see that stinkin' breed son of a bitch, I'll drill a hole right between his goddamned eyes. He used to ride for me. Now he's out huntin' my hide."

"Why?"

Dutch Schultz stood up and stepped over to the window, peering out through the dirty glass for several seconds. Then he reached over to his bunk and picked up a half-empty bottle of Montana red-eye. Uncorking the top, he lifted the bottle to his lips and took a few gulps, then offered the bottle to Cavannagh. Cavannagh shook his head.

"Cy Moore picks this stuff up for me when he's in Benton. Helps pass the time."

Schultz lifted one of the Winchesters, sat back down on the rickety chair, and laid the rifle across the table.

"The night you saw me in that Sioux camp, I arranged to meet Crooked Moon and his warriors at Medicine Lodge Coulee where I'd give 'em Winchesters for Black Hills gold. The only trouble with that arrangement was me and the boys got to Medicine Lodge Coulee early an' them damned Minnetarees turned up ahead of the Sioux an' took the guns for themselves. If you hadn't barged into their camp all dressed up in a red coat like you was the Great White Mother's number one soldier chief himself, they'd have killed me just like they did the rest of my boys."

Schultz took another swig of Montana red-eye.

"I didn't figger that deal out all by myself. I had a partner. He arranged for the Winchesters. My part was the risky bit, gettin' 'em to Crooked Moon."

"So he could attack Fort Walsh," Cavannagh interjected pointedly.

"Do you wanna listen, or would you rather give me a lecture?" Schultz asked impatiently.

"Go on."

Schultz nipped at the red-eye again and wiped his sleeve across his hairy mouth. "Half that gold Crooked Moon was supposed to give me was to have been mine, the other half I was to give my partner. Well, when I couldn't give it to him because I didn't have it, he figgered I double-crossed him. He didn't believe me about the Minnetarees beatin' the Sioux to the rifles. He figgered I was holdin' out on him, so he sent his guns to get me. I been on the dodge ever since, until Cy let me hole up out here."

Schultz's hands tightened around his Winchester. "The thing that singes my ass about that goddamned Buffalo Johnny is that he was supposed to be with us in our camp at Medicine Lodge when the Minnetarees hit us. The son of a bitch skipped out on me, almost

83

like he knew them Minnetarees was comin'."

Schultz got to his feet and peered out the window for several seconds, then returned to the rickety chair.

"I've done a piece of talkin', Cavannagh. Mostly all you done is ask questions." He pointed at Cavannagh's light blue cavalry breeches. "Hard to break old habits, I see. If you're still in the Mounted Police up in Canada, how come you're down here in Montana?"

When Cavannagh told him, Schultz burst into laughter. "So you figgered I was ramroddin' this army-raidin' operation?"

"I thought you might be."

"An' you figgered you could come ridin' in and ask me all about it. You're either plumb loco or you just like livin' dangerous-like."

"I was counting on our friendship."

Schultz shook his head in wonderment. "Cavannagh, you gotta be the boldest son of a bitch I ever set eyes on."

Undaunted, Cavannagh asked, "Have you ever heard of a red-bearded Irishman named Michael O'Shaugnessy?"

"No."

"William Meldrum?"

"I knew a Bill Meldrum in Benton."

"About forty, droopy moustache. Claims he killed a few men in the war."

"That'd be the same one, but the only way he killed any men would've been back a piece from the real fighting. He was in the artillery."

"I arrested him with two wago. just north of the border."

"He should've known better'n to ge was peddlin' rotgut out of Fort Whoop-U Mounted Police came into the country. Him whole outfit pulled back into Montana as so they found out the redcoats were coming. All except old Dave Akers. He stayed."

"Meldrum wasn't very happy to be arrested. He and his outfit would still be in the Fort Walsh guardhouse if Michael O'Shaughnessy hadn't paid their fines to the tune of sixteen hundred dollars."

Schultz let out a long whistle. "Must of figgered they was pretty good men."

Cavannagh picked up his Winchester and handed it to Schultz. "They had ten of these. Look familiar?"

Schultz turned the rifle over in his hands. "Looks like any other Winchester '73 .44-40." He passed it back.

"It looks like part of that shipment you were running to the Indians."

"What're you gettin' at?"

"That this Winchester and the ones you were running came from the same place."

"I guess they all do when you come right down to it."

Cavannagh leaned forward over the table. "Look, Dutch . . . two lots of brand-new Winchesters . . . that half-breed Buffalo Johnny, first working for you, then for Meldrum, now out hunting you, acting as a gun for your former partner. Don't you see a hultz frowned. "So? He worked for me, then he finds a job workin' for Meldrum, then when Meldrum gets arrested, the stinkin' breed son of a bitch gets himself hired somewheres else."

Cavannagh looked disappointed. "I thought you were a suspicious man, Dutch. How about that one-time partner of yours employing Meldrum as well?"

"To peddle whisky?" Schultz shook his head. "Naw! He wouldn't be interested in that."

"Why would Michael O'Shaughnessy put up sixteen hundred dollars to pay fines for half a dozen whisky peddlers?"

"You're a policeman, Cavannagh. You figger it out. I got my hands full just stayin' alive." Schultz went back to the window.

"You've got a good ten years on me, Dutch, and you've been in some tight places, so I don't have to tell you this, but I've learned something about staying alive—it helps to know who your enemies are."

Schultz stepped back to the table and drained the bottle of red-eye. "You're talkin' over my head."

"The whisky's fogging your brain."

"You better saddle up and ride the hell outta here. Those guns after me will be after you if they know you're a friend of mine."

"I know. I saw what they would've done to Moore."

"Yeah. I guess mebbe I should pull out. I don't wanna make things difficult for Cy. We been friends a long ways back."

"It could be too late to pull out, Dutch. Too late to

save Cy trouble. Those guns know he's a friend of yours. They might be back, depending upon how bad they want you, and it seems your ex-partner wants you bad enough. Tell me who he is, Dutch. He might be involved in what I'm looking into."

Schultz hesitated before answering. "I can't do that."

Cavannagh regarded Schultz coldly. "You *can't—* or you *won't?*"

"I can't!"

"Why not?"

"Because I don't know him."

Cavannagh stared at Schultz with undisguised surprise.

Schultz looked sheepish. "I know it sounds crazy, but that's the way it was. All the contact I had with him was through a go-between. I guess he wanted to protect his identity."

"How did you get dragged into a deal like that?"

Schultz took a deep breath. "Back in the spring me and my outfit was hangin' around Benton. We'd planned tradin' a little rotgut to the Bloods an' mebbe shootin' a few buffalo, but we hadn't figgered on the Mounted Police bein' as active as they was, especially as they were still so new in the West. As it turned out, we were dead wrong, because they were makin' things pretty unhealthy for the whisky trade. So when this feller I'd seen around off an' on asked me if I was interested in makin' some money, I jumped in. The job happened to be runnin' guns to the Sioux. The pay bein' gold, I didn't see how we could miss provided we were careful. This feller was the go-between for me and the man I reckoned was goin' to be my partner. That's what it was supposed to be — a partnership. He set the thing up and provided the guns. I took the risks and delivered 'em."

Schultz shook his head slowly. "It wasn't a good deal. It cost me my outfit and damned near my life. And it might cost that before I see another birthday."

"Your outfit couldn't have been bigger than three or four men when you were planning to trade rotgut."

"Four."

"But your outfit was bigger than that when I saw you in the Sioux camp."

"I took on some extra hands to look after the extra wagons."

"Buffalo Johnny must have been one of them. He wasn't with you when I first ran into you on the Milk."

"What are you gettin' at?"

"What I've been getting at all along. Buffalo Johnny was a plant. He's worked for this so-called partner of yours all the time. And I think Meldrum is working for him, and the red-bearded Irishman, O'Shaugnessy."

Schultz stood up and yawned. "All this is makin' me plumb tired, Cavannagh. Or mebbe it's the whisky, like you said. Anyways, I need a sleep. On your way to wherever you're goin', I'd appreciate if you'd do a sweep of the countryside. If you see any sign of anyone headin' in my direction, let off three shots from that Winchester you got."

Cavannagh nodded and extended his hand. "So long, Dutch. Good luck."

Schultz grinned, reminding Cavannagh of the Dutch Schultz he used to know. They shook hands.

"So long, Lieutenant. You stick that nose of yours where I think you're gonna stick it, good luck to you. You'll need it."

Winchester in hand, Cavannagh stepped out from the line shack into the bright sunlight beyond.

Chapter 8

Fort Benton had never seen anything like it, and the mixed collection of transients and permanent inhabitants on the dusty main street were making the most of it as two oddly dressed strangers rode by.

"What in tarnation are they?" a grizzly old plainsman asked a bearded man standing next to him on the board sidewalk.

"Damned if I know," the sunken-cheeked prospector replied.

"Must be a circus comin' inter town," a flowing-haired buffalo hunter put in, his long-barreled Sharps over his shoulder.

Someone else let out a catcall, which was followed by peals of laughter.

But the two strangers walked their horses unconcernedly along the street, seemingly impervious to the attention they were getting or the insulting laughter.

"What sorta saddles they settin' on?" a cowboy asked.

"Dunno," a blue-shirted soldier answered. "Even the army don't use saddles like that."

"They got rifles, too. Wonder if they know which

end the bullets come outta."

There were more peals of raucous laughter.

At last one of the strangely dressed men turned his head as if to answer but the other, riding stirrup-to-stirrup beside him, leaned over and jabbed an elbow into his ribs.

The one who had turned his head wore a black bowler hat, a dark gray three-piece suit that he could squeeze into only if he held his breath, a blue-striped white shirt with a stiff white (and travel-dirtied) wing collar, a red-dotted, royal blue tie with a flashy imitation diamond stickpin, shiny (but dusty) black shoes, and buttoned gray spats. A pair of gentlemen's gray dress gloves completed his ensemble. The only article missing to make him resemble the common conception of a London gentlemen was a furled umbrella.

The rib-jabber riding with him wore a predominantly red Royal Stuart tartan tam-o'-shanter complete with bright red pompon on his head, a crimson ascot around his neck, a Scottish tweed hunting jacket, jodhpurs, and riding boots. He was no less an unusual sight in this Montana frontier town than his bowler-hatted companion.

"There's no doubt they belongs to a circus. They looks like trained monkeys sittin' on them things what looks like saddles."

More laughter followed this jibe.

Their saddles differed from the common California stock saddle, the McClellan, or the occasional shiny-spangled Mexican variety. They were pancake flat, with steel stirrups and too many straps and buckles.

And the two riders sat very stiff on them, rigid-backed, their right arms hanging stiffly by their sides.

"Hey, round-head," an unshaven onlooker yelled, standing against a store front, "are yew really ridin' thet hoss, or is the poor critter wearin' its ass up on top o' its back?"

Howls of laughter.

The bowler-hatted Londoner gritted his teeth and spoke with a decided Cockney accent to his companion in the Royal Stuart tam-o'-shanter.

"One more bleedin' shout like that an' I'm gunna get horff this bleedin' 'orse an' deck some bah-stard, Sar'nt."

"Noo ye nae, Freddie," the other replied in a deep Scots burr. "Just pretend ye're ridin' wi' a mounted column through some mutinous village in the bluidy Punjab."

"Me bleedin' imagination hain't hup to it. At least there the bah-stards kept their bleedin' traps shut, an' even if they had of opened 'em, you couldn't bleedin' well understand 'em anyway."

"Ye bear in mind what we're doon here for. The major said he wanted nae trouble. He was verra definite aboot tha'."

The Cockney grunted. "Orright. I'll make a special effort to contain meself. At that, I should save it for them bah-stards back in barracks what told me this was a bit of a toff's town."

Colin Campbell MacGregor snorted. "I'm surprised ye believed tha' rubbish. Ye should've known better. Have ye nae read any of them Ned Buntline penny dreadfuls? This is the American frontier, laddie."

They rode a little further in silence, ignoring the derisive shouts and amused stares, until the Cockney pointed excitedly. "Look, Sar'nt—dancing girls! Now, that's more like it." He drew back his arm, straightened his flashy tie, and adjusted his coat.

Sergeant McGregor saw the half-dozen painted dancing girls lined in front of a dance hall flashing smiles at them.

"The boys in barracks weren't lyin' after all. At least, not about that. Let's find a place for the 'orses an' in we goes."

"Hold it, Freddie. We're here to find Cavannagh."

"Stuff Cavannagh! I lost me bleedin' corporal's stripes because of him. 'e's probably deserted now 'e's back in 'is own bleedin' country. Come on, Sar'nt. This is what I got dressed up like this for—dancin' girls!"

"Ye lost your stripes for telling lies aboot Cavannagh, and because Cavannagh is the better man of the two of ye. And ye got dressed up like that because we were told tae wear civilian clothes and that suit is the only civilian clothing ye own."

"It's me best suit. Got it for me sister's weddin' back in London town four year ago."

They rode on past the dance hall, Freddie "Cockney" Jenkins giving it a lingering look as they put it behind them. At the next corner MacGregor saw a livery stable and led them to it. That at least got them away from the looks and jeers, although the livery keeper couldn't keep his eyes off these two oddly dressed men. But he recognized that they certainly knew horses as he watched them remove their coats, take off their saddles, and settle down to currycomb and brush their mounts.

Half an hour later they were back on Front Street, this time on foot, Freddie strutting in his bowler hat and tight, out-of-place suit as though he were promenading around Piccadilly Circus instead of Fort Benton, Montana.

"Here's that dancin' hall again, Sar'nt. What about a little 'op inside? Do us both a spot of good."

Sergeant MacGregor firmly shook his head. "Nae yet, Freddie. It's a wee bit early."

"How about a whorehouse? I think I spotted one of 'em across the corner from the stables."

They were attracting attention again. Men passing them on the sidewalk turned to look behind them and snickered.

Even under his black bowler, Freddie was a rock-faced, lantern-jawed man with a mean look, and only hard-fisted, rough-living men should have had the nerve to make insulting remarks, especially when passing within reaching distance. But men living on the frontier were often prone to dangerous rashness.

"It ain't a circus. It's a vaudeville show comin' to town. On'y vaudeville actors would have the gol-danged gall t' dress like thet."

Freddie clenched his fists and was about to turn on the passerby who had made that remark, but Sergeant MacGregor grabbed his arm. "Hold your temper, Freddie. We're in a foreign country and we have tae behave oorselves."

Freddie growled but went along quietly. After a

moment he asked, "Where the bleedin' 'ell are we goin', anyway?"

"Looking for Cavannagh."

Freddie made a face. "And where the bleedin' 'ell might 'e be?"

"I dinna know, but we'll start with the I. G. Baker store. I recall passing it when we rode by. I think it's the big white-fronted place up the street opposite those riverboats."

"How about a quick drink first, just to wet the old whistle?" Freddie pointed to a set of swing doors. "There's a pub right there, Sar'nt. Made to order."

MacGregor scowled. "All right, but just one."

And in they went.

Unlike MacGregor, Freddie Jenkins had never read any Buntline westerns, so he had no preconceived notion of what a western saloon should look like. He had drunk in bars, pubs, canteens, dens, and dives halfway around the world—England, Egypt, India, South Africa, Malta, Canada. They all had two things in common—liquor and customers. This one plainly had the same, which was all that mattered.

They bellied up to the bar and were quick to notice that all noise ceased, save for the occasional clink of a glass. Whatever activity had been taking place immediately prior to their entry had abruptly stopped. Looking into the long, bottle-lined mirror on the wall behind the polished counter, MacGregor saw that the saloon's twenty or thirty patrons, sitting at the dozen or more tables spread around the room, a couple of others lounging at the bar, all had their eyes glued to Jenkins and him.

A beefy, bald-headed bartender chomping on a cigar ambled along behind the bar and stopped in front of them. "What'll it be?"

MacGregor smiled pleasantly. "What hae ye got?"

"Whisky" was the gruff reply.

"All right, make it whisky." MacGregor turned his head sideways. "How aboot ye, Freddie?"

Freddie tilted his bowler forward over his right eyebrows. "Yeah—whisky."

The bartender poured two drinks. "That'll be two dollars."

MacGregor peered at him across the bar. "*Two dollars*? Is tha' nae a little steep?"

The beefy bartender held on to the two glasses. "You want 'em or not?"

MacGregor reached into his pocket and plunked two silver dollars onto the counter. The bartender released the two glasses and picked up the silver coins.

Lifting their glasses, the two men tossed the amber liquid down their throats.

"*Jesus!*" Freddie spat, clutching his throat while slamming down his glass onto the counter. "That tasted like undiluted horse piss! If that's the bleedin' stuff you Yankees peddle to the ruddy Indians, it's no bleedin' wonder it rots their bleedin' guts!"

"Shut up, Freddie," MacGregor growled. "Dinna offend these people."

But in the stilled silence of the long room, everyone in the saloon heard the remark, for Freddie had made no effort to keep his voice down.

The bartender opened his mouth to say something,

but a gravel voice from one of the tables behind MacGregor and Jenkins beat him to it.

"Eff'n yew cain't drink men's likker, dude, yew shouldna oughta be in a place like this!"

Freddie whirled around but MacGregor planted a large hairy hand on the Cockney's shoulder and whirled him back again.

"Settle down, Freddie. Hae another drink. I'm buyin'."

MacGregor reached into the pocket for two more silver dollars and plunked them down on the bar, pointing to the two glasses, which the bartender refilled.

A murmur of subdued conversation gradually filled the saloon, but occasionally some of it reached their ears.

"Mebbe they rode down from Canada. I hear tell there's lots o' Scotchmen up there. What d' they call it . . . the Hudson's Bay Company? Lots o' Scotchmen up at them tradin' forts."

"Wherever they comes from, they're sure a powerful argument for immigration laws."

Laughter.

"We shoulda marched right up on thar back in '70, afore they marked the border, and turned all that part of Canada into American territory."

MacGregor heard that and quickly glanced into the mirror. He couldn't see who had made the remark but it offended his imperial sentiments. The atmosphere was becoming uncomfortable. It was time to leave.

"Whadda they call them things Scotchmen wear on their heads? Bonnets, ain't it?"

Plainly a tableful of Missouri men were bent on some fun.

"Mebbe he ain't a Scotchman. I allus allowed Scotchmen wore skirts. Unless he's got one on under his trousers."

"Naw," guffawed another. "They don't wear trousers. Jes' skirts, an' under them they don't wear nuthin'."

A loud outburst of laughter greeted that remark.

Face reddening, MacGregor said to Freddie, "Let's get oot of here."

But Freddie was spoiling for a fight.

"Let's leave these bah-stards something to remember us by, Sar'nt."

MacGregor shook his head sharply. "Noo—noo trouble." He turned to go.

A one-eyed Missouri man stuck out his boot and blocked MacGregor's way. "Leavin' so soon, immygrant?"

MacGregor stared back at his one green eye. "Tha' we are," he said evenly and pushed the man's boot out of the way.

The one-eyed man drew a gun and fired a shot into the plank floor an inch in front of the big Scot's foot. MacGregor stopped short.

"Hey!" shouted the bartender.

The one-eyed Missouri man waved the bartender's protest aside. "We're jes' goin' t' have a little entertainment, Frank. Thar won't be no damage done." He laughed brutally. "Not to the premises, anyway."

The other men sitting around the table, all tough-looking characters wearing six-guns, added their

98

laughter.

MacGregor said calmly, "I'll give ye fair warnin', mon. I'm nae used tae having people shoot in my direction without me doin' something about it."

One of the other Missouri men pulled his long gunmetal-black six-shooter and pointed it at the floor in front of MacGregor's feet. "Thet's a right funny language you talk, immygrant. Let's see iff'n you kin dance as funny as you talk."

He hooked his thumb over the hammer to pull it back, but at that precise instant Freddie launched a lightning kick that caught him beneath his wrist, knocking the wrist up and sending the unhammered six-gun flying.

The man let out a startled yell as Freddie pivoted on his other foot and drove his fist into the side of the man's face. Only a stinging blow, it lacked force but it was unexpected and achieved its purpose.

While One-Eye's attention was distracted, MacGregor stamped the full power of one hundred and ninety pounds down onto his boot. One-Eye let out a scream as pain shot through his instep, but the brawny Scot grabbed him by his shirt collar, yanked him to his feet, and heaved him through the air to the next table.

Freddie didn't wait for the other Missouri men to join in. He smashed his rock-hard fists into their unshaven faces. But now all hell broke loose as hitherto bored patrons sitting at the other tables — frontiersmen, cowpunchers, buffalo hunters, roust-abouts — Missouri men all, whooping wildly, gleefully joined in.

The bald-headed bartender threw down his cigar, bellowing to the men to stop or his barroom would be turned into a shambles.

He was totally ignored as fists hammered and slammed. Freddie punched faces, ribs, bellies, kidneys—anything that got in his way. Someone took a shot at his bowler as it went sailing across the room, and his precious suitcoat was ripped off his back.

A sea of buckskin, flavored with the pungent aroma of horse sweat and unwashed bodies, swarmed around MacGregor. Shouting strange Gaelic oaths and swinging big hairy fists, the brawny Scot tore into the fight. His fist shattered a bony nose, a swinging forearm caught a Missouri man on the side of the head, and another body hurtled through the air.

Cursing, the bartender picked up a shotgun from behind his bar and fired one barrel into the ceiling. Seconds later a chair rocketed across the room and framed his shiny pate between its wooden legs.

Freddie, his vest torn to shreds, his shirt off his back, went down under three or four men, but a minute later he struggled up between flailing arms and kicking legs. MacGregor lifted a heavy table and rammed it into half a dozen men, driving them through the swinging doors into the street outside, which was quickly filling with curious spectators responding to the excited calls of *"Fight! Fight!"*

As MacGregor turned to reenter the saloon a heavy hand fell on his shoulder. Pivoting, the big Scot lashed out with a straight shoulder-thrown left that caught the man full on the jaw and sent him skidding across the dusty street where he came to a stop flat on his back. That he was wearing a dull silver star on his coat only half registered on MacGregor as he charged back inside the saloon.

Eight men had Freddie backed up against the bar, but they were afraid to get closer than a semicircle of six feet because the torn and tattered Cockney had picked up a whisky bottle, smashed the end of it on the polished bar top, and stood waving the jagged neck menacingly at his attackers. One of them was reaching for a holstered six-gun when MacGregor broke a chair over his head from behind.

The other seven turned to meet this new threat, but before they could do anything, MacGregor was into them with his one hundred and ninety pounds of bone and muscle. Now with the odds less uneven, Freddie threw away his weapon and hurled himself into the fray.

Onlookers packed into the doorway, shouting encouragement to the combatants. It was good entertainment, one of the best brawls Fort Benton had seen for a long time.

Freddie saw his black bowler sitting on the floor at the far side of the room and ran across to it. As he knelt down to retrieve it a heavy spurred boot descended upon it and crunched the top flat to the floor.

Freddie's head shot up, his eyes seeking the identity of the perpetrator of this outrage, but before they focused fully a gun barrel struck him on the side of the temple and sent him rolling across the floor.

MacGregor was now alone, facing three Missouri men, all that were left standing of the twenty or thirty who had taken part in the brawl. The brawny Scot stood, his tam long gone from his head, face bleeding, fists balled in front of him.

The three Missouri men slowly moved in on this funny-speaking, grinning madman.

"Oh! Come on, ye wee laddies. Come on tae wee Colin MacGregor so I can smash your bluidy mugs in."

One of the Missouri men reached for a knife.

"Agh! Are ye nae man enough tae tackle me wi'oot a knife, ye scurvy bastard? An' there's three o' ye."

The Missouri man scowled, tossed the knife aside, and dashed in. MacGregor's fist in his face stopped him cold and he fell heavily to the floor. But now the other two hurled themselves at the Scot. MacGregor cracked one of them on the neck with the heel of his open hand and flung the other across the bar top. He whirled just in time to catch the arm of the man who had pistol-whipped Freddie as that arm, still with the pistol at the end of it, was arcing through the air to crush in his skull. Blocking the swing with one arm, MacGregor threw his hip into the man's side, brought up his other arm to just below his adversary's shoulder, grabbed his wrist, and bent the pistol-swinging arm up around the man's back with such force that he screamed in pain and dropped the gun. Grabbing a fistful of his hair, MacGregor jerked the man to the floor.

"Yuh broke my goddamn arm!" he sobbed.

"I didna break it," MacGregor panted. "But ye'll nae be usin' it tae swing a gun barrel for a day or two."

102

The Scot wiped a big hairy paw across his mouth as he staggered back to lean against the bar and rest. His hand was covered in blood. His or someone's else's? He put the other hand up to his mouth, took it away, and looked at it. Bright red blood! His!

He looked around. The saloon was a shambles—broken chairs, tables, bottles, and glasses littered the floor which was sprawled with bodies wherever he looked. A silent crowd hemmed in the swing doors, one of which hung from only one hinge, almost ripped off by the Scot's table-ramming charge.

"*Freddie*! Where are ye, Freddie, lad?"

A groan sounded from the far side of the wrecked saloon. "Oooh. Me bleedin', stuffin' 'ead." Rubbing the side of his head, the Cockney struggled to his feet.

"Come on, Freddie. Let's get the bluidy hell oot of here while the getting's good."

Suddenly something hard was jammed into MacGregor's back, followed by the dull click of a gun hammer being drawn back.

"You ain't goin' nowhere, you goddamn Doomsday son of a bitch! You goddamn wrecked my place, an' by Christ, you're gonna pay for it."

The bartender, part of the broken chair still hanging around his neck, held the double-barrel shotgun in MacGregor's back. One barrel was still full.

A middle-aged man, heavy moustache above a wide mouth, picked his way through the crowd at the door. A dull silver star was pinned to his coat and he held a hand to his jaw. His other hand reached for a six-shooter at his hip.

"It's all right, Frank," he said to the bartender. "He ain't goin' nowhere but my jail. I got a score to settle with him."

The bartender waved his shotgun at Freddie on the other side of the saloon. "That other son of a bitch, too, Sheriff. He was the one what started all the goddamn trouble."

"Is that so? Then I'll take him as well. They can both cool their asses in Crowbar Hotel."

will it arroive here?"

The clerk scratched his head. "Well, Big Muddy is running a bit low," he replied slowly. "Lot of sandbars on the bends . . . haven't had the summer rains we normally get . . . *Fontanna*'s pretty heavily loaded . . . she only draws two feet of water, but the river's a lot less than that in places . . . not much more than a foot . . ."

"Get to the point!" the Irishman prodded impatiently.

The clerk frowned in annoyance. "What I'm trying to say is that there's a good chance the *Fontanna* will unload all of its cargo at Cow Island."

"And were, moight oi ask, is that?"

"Sixty miles downriver, give or take a mile."

"And what happens there? To the freight, oi mean."

"The Baker Company sends its wagons down there and brings the stuff here to Benton. Or in the case of the Canadian merchandise—"

The Irishman held up his hand. "Thank you. Say no more." Grinning widely, he pushed away from the counter and strode across the floor to the door. Before opening it, he turned to the clerk and waved. "Thank you . . . and good day, sorr."

Two riders splashed their lathering horses across a shallow stream, climbed them up an embankment, and urged them into a canter along a sweeping, richly grassed plateau. The Cypress Hills rose out of the ground behind them. Ahead in the blue-haze distance loomed a range of rocky hills.

"Dat d' Bear Paws, *mon Capitaine*," one of the riders, a bearded, shaggy-haired *Metis* shouted over the noise of pounding hoofs, pointing a buckskin-covered arm. Then he swung his arm to the left and pointed again. "Dat's a border marker, what d' In'ians call *stone heaps*. Once we pass dat, we in American territory."

The other rider didn't bother replying. Young at twenty-seven, with a neatly trimmed blond moustache, he was new to the West but not uninformed. He knew what the rock cairn signified and he had heard Major Walsh refer to them as *stone heaps*, markers of the medicine line, over which columns of blue-coated American troops wouldn't chase fleeing parties of war-painted Sioux or horse-stealing Bloods.

They put the stone border marker behind them and penetrated Montana. After riding a further two miles the *Metis* veered half left, heading southeast.

"We keep d' Bear Paws on our right, *mon Capitaine*."

Douglas Gordon Fraser veered his horse half left to keep pace with the *Metis* scout. Then he shouted at him.

"Stop calling me *Captain*, Prefontaine. That's not my rank. Besides, as I am wearing civilian clothes and we are now in American territory, it would be more appropriate for you to address me as *Mister* Fraser."

Sitting easily in his rocking saddle, swaying with the motion of his cantering horse, Jules Prefontaine merely shrugged. He hadn't missed the rebuff in the other's tone and inwardly it galled him that instead of riding with his friend Cavannagh, wherever he was, he had to guide this arrogant young sub-inspector on a seemingly urgent journey across dangerous Sioux country all the way down to the Missouri.

Chapter 10

The wide western sky hung low, a flat gray ceiling pressing down on a deflated John Tarlton Cavannagh as he rode his bay across the rolling prairie back to Fort Benton.

He had been so sure he would pick up enough information from Dutch Schultz to put him on the trail of the outlaws responsible for raiding army munitions wagons. Instead, he had learned nothing. He was right back where he had been when he left Fort Walsh a week ago. Worse! Then he had a starting point. Now he didn't even have that.

He had been sure Schultz would have known something about the red-bearded Irishman, O'Shaughnessy. That he didn't was a major disappointment in itself.

Michael O'Shaughnessy — that name haunted Cavannagh. And the pale, red-bearded face that went with it. Paying sixteen hundred dollars, more than Cavannagh would earn in five years as a Mounted Police corporal, to get six Missouri outlaws out of jail, then allegedly hiring them to escort him west through Blackfoot country to the Rocky Mountains while he looked into the business of setting up trading posts. Tradings posts — *hell!* It had been their tracks Cavannagh and Jules had spotted heading south for Montana, where they had met up at the campsite with three mysterious riders, one of whom wore moccasins like an Indian or a half-breed. Buffalo Johnny, undoubtedly! All taking pains to keep off the regular trail, out of sight of redcoat patrols.

Then there were those Winchester repeaters, all identical, all brand-new. The same as the ones Dutch Schultz had been running. There was a connection, Cavannagh was sure, despite what Schultz said. There had to be.

The common thread running through all this was Buffalo Johnny. First with Schultz, then with Meldrum, now with the gunmen looking for Schultz. One thing — that half-breed wouldn't be wearing that ridiculous black stovepipe hat again. Actually, Cavannagh wished he hadn't shot it off Buffalo Johnny's head the day before yesterday at Moore's homestead. Now he would be harder to spot the next time — and Cavannagh knew very well there would be a next time.

Fort Benton's main street was bustling with activity — rumbling wagons, cracking whips, cussing bullwhackers, clattering horsemen. Cavannagh, walking his bay through this typical frontier settlement traffic, glanced over at the riverboat docks, his eyes under his dark blue cavalry hat brim squinted against the sun's glare as it tried to break through thick clouds. It hurt his eyes, but before turning his head away, he noticed there were only two sternwheelers

111

docked now.

Outside the sheriff's office, Cavannagh swung down out of his saddle and looped the bay's reins to a hitching rail. Inside he found the sheriff sitting at a battered desk perusing a list of local residents who hadn't paid their taxes.

"Howdy, young fella," the sheriff said, looking up. "Didn't find that Schultz character, did you?"

Cavannagh reported the deaths of the two gunmen at Moore's homestead but omitted any mention of Dutch Schultz. Just as he finished up, he casually glanced over at the cells in the corner and saw two scowling faces peering at him through the bars. At first he didn't recognize the bruised and bloodied features, especially as this was the last place he would have expected to find them, but then he burst out laughing.

"I dinna see anything tae bluidy well laugh aboot!"

The sheriff frowned. "You know them?"

Tears streaming down his cheeks, Cavannagh nodded. "Yes, I know them. What are they in here for?"

"They damned near wrecked a saloon on Front Street. They're due for a personal appearance before Judge Harvey on twenty-nine counts of assault and battery on citizens of the Territory of Montana—thirty charges, that is, countin' that chair one of 'em wrapped around Frank the barkeep's head—"

"We dinna wrap any chair around his head," Mac-Gregor's growl interrupted.

The sheriff's face clouded with annoyance as he snapped over his shoulder at the cells. "Shut up back there!" Turning back to Cavannagh, he added, "Then there's the cost of repairin' the damage to the saloon."

"Ye'll nae be hangin' all tha' on us," MacGregor barked from the bars.

"I said shut up back there!" the sheriff's voice grated irritably. Again he resumed talking to Cavannagh. "That, together with whatever fines Judge Harvey figgers is proper . . . well, unless they got lots of money—which I know they ain't—they're gonna be behind bars a long time. Prob'ly they'll wind up in the territorial prison."

Cavannagh did some fast thinking. He didn't know why MacGregor and Jenkins were in Fort Benton. Perhaps Major Walsh had given them a few days leave. Whatever the reason, they were here in jail and in trouble, something Major Walsh wouldn't want. It was up to him to get them out of it.

"Do you know who these two men are, Sheriff?"

"No. They won't say."

Cavannagh fixed his steely blue eyes on the law officer. "Are you a patriotic man, Sheriff?"

His long face a question mark, the sheriff tilted himself back in his chair and looked up at the tall, dark young man in army blue. "I reckon I am."

"Well, that pair back there are two of the finest fighting soldiers ever to wear a uniform. Colonel Custer himself wants to take them on in the Seventh Cavalry. You know how things are now that the Sioux and Cheyenne are threatening to take the warpath. All of Montana could be caught up in it. Benton itself could be overrun in one great angry wave. The only thing that can prevent it is the army. The army needs men like those two."

The sheriff rubbed his whiskers and looked thoughtful.

Cavannagh continued. "Another thing you should know about them — they're experts at breaking out of prisons. In fact, I'm surprised they're still there. Why, there's not a military prison in the country that can hold them. And they make a hell of a mess when they break out."

A worried expression clouded the sheriff's face.

Cavannagh moved in for the kill. "You have to keep them here until you can bring them before a judge. Then you've got to escort them to the territorial prison. All that time you have to worry about them kicking the hell out of your jail or escaping on the trail. I can save you all that trouble by taking them to Colonel Custer's headquarters at Fort Lincoln, guaranteeing they'll be off your hands. After all, Sheriff, if the government has to support them, it may as well get its money's worth."

The sheriff sighed and reached for his keys. "You got 'til sundown, young fella, to get them the hell outta town. If they ain't, I'm roundin' up a posse . . ."

"Mon,' ye're a bluidy liar, Cavannagh, if I ever saw one," MacGregor said to Cavannagh as the three men sat eating in a restaurant a stone's throw from the riverboat landing.

Cavannagh forked a slice of beefsteak and held it poised in front of his mouth. "What did you expect me to tell the sheriff? That you're Mounted Policemen from Fort Walsh? After what you did in that saloon, Major Walsh would have your stripes. Anyway, what are you doing in Benton?"

"The major sent us tae give ye a hand. He thought ye might need it."

Cavannagh finished chewing. "Put another way, you're to restrain me."

The big Scot laughed. "Tae be blunt, laddie . . . the major knows you're a guid mon, but ye're a wee bit likely tae take matters into your own hands, so upon reflection he thought it wise tae send me, a sergeant, tae make sure ye dinna bite off more than ye could chew. Freddie's along just in case we need a wee bit of weight. Hae ye found oot anything?"

Cavannagh shook his head.

As they ate, some of the restaurant's other customers cast frequent glances at their table, for MacGregor and Freddie had attained a measure of temporary fame in Fort Benton. Despite the western clothing they had just bought from the I. G. Baker store (although the brawny Scot refused to discard his Royal Stuart tam-o'-shanter), their battered faces were recognizable badges.

Upon finishing, they were about to step out through the restaurant door when Cavannagh's jaw dropped. For a moment he could hardly believe his eyes.

On the far side of the street, the side next to the muddy Missouri, walked three men. One wore a tall black stovepipe hat! The second sported a flaming red beard. The third was half-hidden by the other two, but what Cavannagh could see of him looked decidedly familiar.

An elbow nudged Cavannagh in the ribs. "Ye look like ye're in a trance."

"I'll be damned!" Cavannagh muttered. Then,

without a word of explanation, he bounded out the door.

The three men walked toward the riverboat landing. A third stern-wheeler had arrived, taking its place behind the other two. Passengers were disembarking and deckhands prepared deck cargo for unloading.

"Where are ye going?" MacGregor asked, catching up to Cavannagh.

"Those three men across the street," Cavannagh replied. "That one in the middle, the one with the red beard, he was at Fort Walsh when I took in those whisky peddlers. The half-breed under that stovepipe, he was their lookout. I shot that hat off his head the other day, or one just like it. He must have bought a new one."

Cavannagh and MacGregor, with an unusually silent Freddie Jenkins behind them, followed the three men to the third riverboat, still puffing a thin stream of smoke skyward from its twin stacks. The trio pushed their way up the gangway onto the main deck, threaded past passengers, and climbed a stairway to the upper deck.

It was then that Cavannagh recognized the third man—William Meldrum, the droopy-moustached leader of the whisky peddlers he arrested, the man who threatened to kill him if he ever returned to Montana.

On the upper deck, led by Michael O'Shaughnessy, the three disappeared through a doorway.

Watching from the landing, Cavannagh said, "I'm going aboard to see where they went. You two stay here."

Glancing up, Cavannagh read the nameplate on the upper-deck railing: *Minerva Belle*. From the gangway he alighted onto the deck, then moved among disembarking passengers to the upper-deck stairway. Taking the stairs three at a time, he legged it along the upper deck toward the doorway through which O'Shaughnessy and his two companions had gone. But before he could reach it, half a dozen burly deckhands, three of them muscular Negroes, ambled along the deck and spread themselves out to block his way.

Cavannagh stopped.

The half-dozen deckhands stood, arms folded across their chests, knives at their belts, staring at the lone man in fringed buckskin jacket and blue cavalry hat. No one said a word.

Cavannagh moved to go around one of the big deckhands but another stepped immediately in front of him, his nose no more than three inches from Cavannagh's. From nowhere he produced a hard, round belaying pin.

The others pushed forward to mill around the lone man in buckskin and blue, but Cavannagh stepped quickly back out of reach. Their intent was plain. There was nothing Cavannagh could do but get the hell away from there.

From the landing dock Cavannagh walked away along the dusty street and took a circuitous route down alleys and around the backs of buildings until he rejoined MacGregor and Jenkins at the corner of a hardware store where they could not be seen from the *Minerva Belle*.

"We saw wha' happened," MacGregor said. "Freddie and I could go aboard and create a diversion while ye get back up there and look around."

"Yeah," grinned Freddie, his taste for another brawl overcoming his dislike for Cavannagh. "They're big bastards, but there's only six of 'em."

"Remember the sheriff," Cavannagh cautioned. "That's all he'd need. I've got to find out what those three are up to, but we'll have to wait until they come back off board."

They waited until after dark before O'Shaughnessy, Meldrum, and Buffalo Johnny left the *Minerva Belle*. In the darkness they might have missed them altogether if Cavannagh hadn't spotted the telltale silhouette of the half-breed's stovepipe hat.

They followed them along the street, and when the trio crossed from the shadows on the river side to the yellow shafts beaming out from the saloons, dancing halls, and gambling dens, Cavannagh expected them to seek entertainment. Instead, they continued toward the end of town where the livery stables were located.

Snatches of conversation drifted back. Cavannagh was desperately anxious to hear what they were saying, and when they turned into one of the stables, he whispered urgently to Sergeant MacGregor.

"They're pulling out of town, Mac. We have to follow them. You and Jenkins get our horses. I'll try and get close to them."

With that, he sprinted silently ahead to the stable, where, after some reconnoitering he found a ladder at the back leading to a hayloft. Soundlessly praying that the loft would be open, he mounted the ladder and went stealthily up the rungs. Above the top rung was a small man-door. Holding his breath in hopeful anticipation, he grasped the bottom of the door with his fingers and pulled. It gave, and swung open with a slight creak. Instantly he stopped its swing and listened tensely. Hearing nothing from inside the stable, he concluded that the noise had been so slight that it couldn't have been heard by anyone inside, and he swung the door open wider. It creaked again but no louder than before. When it was open wide enough, Cavannagh got his hand inside, grabbed the wall, and hauled himself up. Once inside, he reached out and carefully pulled the door shut behind him.

He waited until his eyes adjusted to the blackness inside the hayloft. There was light reflected from the main part of the stable below at the other end and carefully feeling around, he crept forward through the hay on hands and knees.

At the edge of the loft he could look down on two rows of stalls, about eight or nine on each side, with an aisle perhaps seven feet wide running down the center. Meldrum and Buffalo Johnny stood saddling their horses in stalls side by side. O'Shaughnessy was further back, closer to the loft. They seemed to be alone in the stable and O'Shaughnessy and Meldrum were talking, not loudly, but Cavannagh could hear them plainly enough.

"It's a measure of the Colonel's confidence in you, Meldrum me friend, that he allowed you into the cabin to talk to him. It's a privilege he bestows on only a precious few, oi'll tell you."

"Was he really a colonel durin' the war?"

"Oi don't know, nor does it matter."

Meldrum belched. The sound carried clearly up to Cavannagh's ears, Meldrum followed it by asking, "What was the Colonel so het up about Clay an' Jiggs for?"

"They bungled killing Schultz. The Colonel doesn't like bunglers."

"How come he didn't git upset none at Buffalo Johnny?"

From his lofty perch Cavannagh saw the halfbreed's tall black hat jerk up, the evil dark face completely devoid of expression, the black eyes glittering, and a chill crept over him.

O'Shaughnessy was slipping on his horse's bridle. "Buffalo Johnny's an old friend of the Colonel's."

"A spy, huh?"

Cavannagh thought he detected a note of bitter sarcasm in Meldrum's voice.

When O'Shaughnessy didn't answer, Meldrum said, "If'n I ever catch Buffalo Johnny a spyin' on me, I'll fix him up proper-like n' hand him over to the Sioux. They don't like Crows none, not even half-Crows." Adding weight to his words, Meldrum whipped out his .44 and meaningfully twirled it with his finger through the trigger guard a few times before ramming it back into its holster. "No wonder he didn't stick around Schultz's camp when the Sioux were supposed to lift Schultz's hair instead of givin' him gold fer rifles. Anyways, Schultz would've deserved to lose his scalp. He should of know'd better than to think them murderin' savages would give a white man gold from the Black Hills, not even fer rifles. Them Black Hills is Sioux sacred burial."

Cavannagh watched O'Shaughnessy lead his horse out of the stall and along the aisle to the front doors through which the three had entered the stable. The Irishman said something to the Missouri man but this time it didn't carry back clearly to Cavannagh. Meldrum answered with another belch and followed O'Shaughnessy outside. The last thing Cavannagh saw was the rump and swishing tail of Buffalo Johnny's horse and the black-vested back of the half-breed as he pigeon-toed along behind the other two.

Cavannagh rose and hurried to the back of the hayloft, pushed open the small door, and climbed down the ladder. Halfway down, he dropped to the ground and darted through the darkness along the wall toward the front of the stable. He was in time to hear the creak of saddle leather as the three mounted up and rode off into the night.

Impatiently Cavannagh looked around for Mac-Gregor and the horses.

Where the hell are they? he swore irritably to himself as precious seconds ticked by. Damn it all! I can't afford to lose these three now.

Chapter 11

An eternity of several minutes passed before Mac-Gregor came pounding up with the horses.

"Where the hell have you been?" Cavannagh asked impatiently.

MacGregor scowled. "We got lost. This bluidy place looks different at night."

Cavannagh sprang up into the saddle. "Let's go! They've already left town. Where's Jenkins?"

MacGregor looked behind him. "Freddie?" he called.

"Comin', bugger it!" A Cockney voice answered from the darkness.

They rode northward out of town at a steady pace, following a well-used bull-train trail. There was no moon to lighten the darkness and Cavannagh strained his eyes for some sight of the three riders somewhere ahead.

They splashed across a river. On the other side Cavannagh dismounted, kneeled down, and brushed a hand along the ground until he felt wet spots.

"They're up ahead." He leaped back into the saddle. "We better be careful. That breed is tricky. We don't want to run into an ambush."

They rode on warily, occasionally stopping while one of them dismounted to press his ear to the ground. The night remained black, the low cloud cover of earlier in the day giving way here and there to clear patches, revealing high in the sky pockets of glittering stars. It would get cold before the morrow's dawn.

For another hour they followed the north trail, crossing another river, barely high enough to wet the horse's hocks. Again the ground on the far side was damp from the hoofs of the three horses ahead.

"We must have covered a dozen miles," Cavannagh said. "Two or three more will take us to the Marias. It's low but they could have trouble finding the ford in the dark. My guess is they'll camp for the night and cross in daylight."

Cavannagh was proven right two miles further on when they suddenly saw the flame of a campfire flare up brightly against the blackness a few hundred yards ahead.

"That's them," Cavannagh said quietly as he and his two companions reined to.

"We'll camp here and watch," said MacGregor.

Daybreak found Cavannagh lying flat across the brown grass peering over a rise, field glasses to his eyes, watching the camp. He could see Meldrum hunched over a fire cooking breakfast while O'Shaughnessy rolled their blankets. But there was no sign of Buffalo Johnny. Then he swung the glasses beyond the camp and saw the black hat closer to the river, together with the half-breed's blankets and saddle.

Cunning devil, Cavannagh thought. He wouldn't have been caught in any surprise attack on the camp.

Sweeping the glasses along the riverbank, Cavannagh was surprised that the river was so low. In the spring the water was so high that the only way across was to ferry.

When O'Shaughnessy, Meldrum, and Buffalo Johnny finished breakfast and broke camp, Sergeant MacGregor bellied down in the long brown grass beside Cavannagh. Cavannagh handed him the field glasses. MacGregor held them to his eyes and paid particular attention to the red-bearded Irishman as he and the other two walked their horses into the Marias.

"Aye . . . I remember him. I dinna get a guid look at him in Benton yesterday, but I see him plainly noo. He was strutting around Fort Walsh like bluidy King Tut a couple or three weeks ago. He was all over the place, admiring how well we'd built it. He even drew some sketches. Told the major he was a wee bit of an artist."

The three riders splashed across the river to the far side, walked their horses up the sloping bank, and followed the trail as it rose northeastward to crest a rise in the rolling prairie and dip down on the other side.

Cavannagh waited several minutes after they disappeared over the rise, then carefully studied its length through the field glasses, looking for Buffalo Johnny's dark head to appear. He wanted to see if those evil black eyes were watching the trail in case they were being followed.

Finally satisfied that the three men weren't suspicious, Cavannagh and his two fellow policemen mounted their horses and followed them. They splattered across the Marias to the far side and trotted briskly up the trail to the yonder rise, where Cavannagh once more used his glasses. The three riders had left the trail and were cantering over broken prairie toward a large outcropping of jumbled rock rising seventy or eighty feet into the air and measuring what Cavannagh estimated to be the best part of a mile in length and half as much wide. Beyond it swept the wide brown curve of the Missouri.

Instead of dogging the three horsemen's tracks, Cavannagh and his two companions struck out toward Big Muddy, keeping below the rise. At intervals of every mile or so, Cavannagh scanned the prairie over the rise to make sure he didn't lose his quarry. The small dust cloud trailing behind them made them easy to trace. That they were up to something was pretty obvious by the fact that they had left the main trial. Where they were going could lead to nowhere but the successful completion of the mission Major Walsh had allowed them to undertake.

After four miles the rise petered out, forcing Cavannagh, MacGregor, and Jenkins to open prairie. They rode hard for half a mile until they reached a dip, which they continued along until they sighted a low hill ahead. At its foot, Cavannagh reined in, jumped down out of his saddle, and loped up the hill's side. Once upon the top, he threw himself down and swept the prairie ahead with his field glasses. Almost immediately he spotted the dust cloud and focused on the three riders. They had changed direction again and were making directly for a cleft in the rock outcropping.

Cavannagh was about to slide down the hill when he suddenly caught a flicker of movement among the rocks above the cleft. He wasn't sure what it was — it had been too indistinct.

He snapped the glasses back to his eyes and trained them on the cleft, then moved them slowly up above it . . . backward . . . forward . . . up — *there it was again!*

He steadied the glasses. Yes, there it was. Pale blue, like a washed-out sky. A man's shirt — the man wearing it kneeling above a long lip a dozen feet above the deep vertical cleft. He held a rifle, the barrel resting on the lip's edge and pointing toward the three approaching horsemen. As the question formed in Cavannagh's mind — had they seen him? — the man stood up and waved, and O'Shaughnessy waved back. The man in the pale blue shirt knelt down again.

Cavannagh put down his glasses a moment and wondered whether that watcher had seen him, MacGregor, and Jenkins as well. From the sanctuary of the hill, Cavannagh swung his glasses over the country behind him, trying to imagine what someone halfway up that mass of rock would be able to see.

When he turned his glasses back onto the three horsemen, they had almost reached the cleft. A minute later they disappeared into it. Cavannagh scanned the rockface to the lip above. He couldn't see the man in the pale blue shirt anymore, but he was sure he was there.

Remaining on the hill for another few minutes, Cavannagh studied the face, side, and top of the jumbled rock mass before lowering the glasses. They he scrambled down the hill to rejoin Sergeant Mac-Gregor and Freddie Jenkins. Briefly he told them what he had seen.

"We'll have to take a chance that rifleman up on the rocks hasn't see us. I'm going to get up into those rocks somehow. There's something very interesting going on over there."

Freddie grunted. "Prob'ly some bleedin' great exotic whorehouse."

Cavannagh looked at the Cockney's granite-hard face, seeking some sign of friendliness, but the brawler's battered mug was expressionless, the stone-gray eyes as unyielding as the face.

"I'm going to ride around to the offside of that outcropping, where that lookout won't see me," Cavannagh said to MacGregor.

"And then what?"

"Climb up the rock and get in from the top."

"Think ye can do it? Climb up the side, I mean? That rock looks pretty smooth tae me."

"On the side facing us it is, but there's broken rock on the northwest side." Cavannagh looked from Sergeant MacGregor to Freddie. "I'll need someone to come with me as far as the rock . . . to look after my horse. I might be up there a long time."

Freddie laughed contemptuously. "You better go, Sar'nt. 'e might 'ave a bad accident if I go with 'im. Then maybe I'd get them corporal's stripes back."

Sergeant MacGregor frowned angrily. "That's enough of tha' sort of talk, Freddie. We'll all three go."

They rode off to the west, the glittering snow-capped peaks of the Rockies thrusting an irregular line against the blue sky less than a hundred miles away. They kept to the low portions of dips and depressions covering the broken prairie, keeping themselves out of sight of the lookout up on the rock mass.

Sergeant MacGregor glanced back over his shoulder. "We're kicking up dust. Tha' lookout will spot it."

Cavannagh replied, "There's a few small herds of buffalo roaming around. He'll probably attribute it to them."

"*If* he dinna already see us."

It took them a long time and they continued reconnoitering with the field glasses before they were able to detour around a wide semicircle and reach the jumbled rock mass from the northwest. The golden ball of sun was high in the sky when Cavannagh stepped down from his saddle and stood looking up at the rough rocky side of the outcropping.

"Dinna look too bad," said Sergeant MacGregor from his saddle. Then he stood in his stirrups, craned his neck forward, and pointed further along the outcropping. "But over there would be better. There's a low ledge that ye could reach easily frae the ground. Ye walk along it a wee bit tae tha' strat, then follow it all the way tae the top."

Cavannagh followed the direction of the sergeant's

arm. He could see that MacGregor was right, and he walked forward for a closer look. When he returned, the brawny Scot was sitting hunched over on the hard ground with his boots and socks off and taping around his bare feet bandages from a field dressing kit he had pulled from his saddlebags.

Before Cavannagh could voice the question forming on his lips, Sergeant MacGregor tossed the kit to him.

"Do the same as I'm doing. This'll give your feet purchase on the rock. Your boots were made for riding horses, nae climbing rock."

Cavannagh took the kit. "I thought I was going alone."

"Well, ye're not. And that's an order. Noo start taping. We nae hae got all bluidy day."

While Cavannagh bandaged his feet, Sergeant MacGregor produced some lengths of rope and tied his and Cavannagh's boots so they could carry them at their belts. Then, after MacGregor had a brief word with Freddie, they walked to the ledge, climbed up onto it, and started making their way up the side of the rock mass.

On the ground below, Freddie unsaddled their horses, hobbled them, and rigged a loose hackamore around each horse's neck that he could quickly tighten to muzzle them into silence if any other horses carrying unwelcome visitors approached. Then he slid a Winchester out of its bucket, levered a shell into the breech, and stood guard. He glanced up at the side of the rock mass. Cavannagh and MacGregor were more than halfway up. Then he scanned the prairie, looking for other horsemen. Instead, he saw a small herd of wandering buffalo, about a dozen in all, and watched them for a time. When he lifted his hard gray eyes to the rock mass again, Cavannagh and the sergeant were gone.

The sun was directly above, beating down warmly for early October, when Corporal Cavannagh and Sergeant MacGregor clambered down among the rocks to the inside of the outcropping.

Like the inside of a giant, drilled-out back tooth, it was hollow, resembling an immense natural arena except that it had rocks and craggy walls instead of stands and seats. The floor was surprisingly flat, with patches of what looked like good pasturage.

But the sight that met Cavannagh's eyes on that arena floor made his mouth gape open!

Eight or nine dirty gray canvas tents clustered the floor toward the end through which O'Shaughnessy, Meldrum, and Buffalo Johnny had entered. A wide, clearly visible trail led in from the rock wall; probably that point marked the inside of the cleft. A large number of men were gathered around the tents and there were cooking fires burning. Several wagons stood here and there, and behind the tents ran a long corral containing twenty or thirty horses. As many again grazed randomly on the pasturage.

Cavannagh and MacGregor carefully concealed themselves among the rocks. While MacGregor took off his bright red tam-o'-shanter and tucked it inside his shirt, Cavannagh readied his field glasses, shaded the lenses with his hands to keep the sun's reflection from them, and held them to his eyes.

"Give those rocks above over on the far side a guid sweep first," MacGregor said into Cavannagh's ear. "Make sure there's nae a lookout drawing a bead on us."

Cavannagh realized he should have allotted that first priority, but he had been too eager to see what was happening below. He followed the sergeant's suggestion, then finding nothing, quickly turned to the scene below. While he did so, MacGregor squinted at the rocks on the far side, the bright midday sun hurting his eyes, as he searched for the glint of sunlight off a rifle barrel, or anything else unusual or ominous.

Cavannagh counted at least thirty-one heavily armed men, all desperadoes, typical products of the post-Civil War Missouri plains, most of them old enough to have fought during the war, men like Meldrum and Dutch Schultz. Trained, experienced fighting men—*dangerous* fighting men. The type likely to be found raiding army supply trains and munitions wagons—the type likely to be selling rifles and bullets to Indians.

He saw Michael O'Shaughnessy standing on the back of a wagon, talking to the armed desperadoes. Leaning against the wagon was Meldrum, and off to the side Buffalo Johnny. Cavannagh couldn't see the half-breed clearly because some boxes on the wagon partly concealed him, but he could see the tall black stovepipe hat—there was no mistaking that.

But it was another man that caught Cavannagh's

attention — an immense, bald-headed man completely clothed in smoke-greased buckskin and holding a long-barreled buffalo gun. He dwarfed all the others in both height and width, and belted around his great bulging belly were, instead of pistols like the others wore, a Sioux scalping knife and a tomahawk. Cavannagh had seen enough *Lakota* scalping knives to be able to spot one through field glasses even at this distance. And he would have sworn the man, if indeed he was a man, was some giant Oriental from somewhere deep within Inner Mongolia if it weren't for his light skin clothing.

Cavannagh passed the glasses to MacGregor. "Take a look at the giant down there — he has a head like an egg."

MacGregor took the glasses and studied the scene below. "Guid god! Looks like the evil genie in *Aladdin and the Magic Lamp*. No wonder they've got wagons. They need one for him alone. Nae horse would hold him."

The sergeant handed back the glasses. "That red-bearded Irishman seems tae be giving them orders. He's certainly doing a lot of talking."

Cavannagh studied the wagons, searching for any indication that they might be stolen U.S. Army property, profits from the raids on army supply trains. But they looked more like the trappings of a brigade of buffalo hunters. Disappointment washed over him. Perhaps these men were legitimate. Piles of buffalo robes on the ground beyond the tents gave other evidence of buffalo hunting. Maybe O'Shaughnessy did represent trading interests. Yet —

Buffalo Johnny . . . Meldrum . . . the conversation in the stables . . . ?"

"Well . . . wha' noo?" asked MacGregor, crouched down in the rocks beside Cavannagh.

"I wonder what I could find out if I got down where those men are—tonight, after dark."

"Ye might learn, at a relatively early age, wha' it's like t' die. I almost found oot a couple of times during my twenty years o' soldiering. Tha' is, of course, assuming those fellows are who ye think they are."

"That's why I'd like to go down there—to find that out."

"Why dinna we simply get the hell oot of here and report all this tae the nearest military post?"

"I wish it were that simple. The trouble is we don't have any evidence. The army can't do a damned thing on my suspicions alone."

MacGregor grunted. Cavannagh resumed watching and saw O'Shaughnessy get down off the wagon and step over to the side with the egg-headed giant where they conferred earnestly. While they talked, a hammer banged noisily against an iron ring and the mass of desperadoes moved over to a chuck wagon. Cavannagh could almost swear he caught the odor of roasted buffalo steaks wafting up from below. MacGregor stirred and took new interest in what was happening down there.

"I'm getting bluidy hungry."

They watched the men below line up for food, and again Cavannagh was struck with the similarity between this gang of Missouri desperadoes and a military body. The same feeling returned that he had had back at the Mounted Police post in the Cypress Hills while listening to Major Walsh briefing B Troop's officers and NCOs on the activities of the raiders. He was now even more convinced that these men below were undeniably the same Missouri raiders.

"Look at that red-bearded pig wolfing that grub doon," MacGregor muttered covetously, his dark eyes seeing plainly enough without the aid of field glasses.

"Fine way to talk about a fellow Celt," Cavannagh chided, but through the glasses he noticed that Meldrum was also eating quickly, while the others were consuming their food at a more leisurely pace. Why were those two hurrying? Were they about to leave?

A few minutes later Cavannagh had his answer as one of the gang brought over two saddled horses, not the two O'Shaughnessy and Meldrum had ridden out on but two fresh ones from the makeshift corral. It was plain that most of the extra horses were spares — just about a spare horse for each man. Traveling that way, the raiders could cover considerable distances pretty quickly.

O'Shaughnessy and Meldrum pulled themselves up into their saddles. But not Buffalo Johnny. He stood near the egg-headed giant, waiting.

Cavannagh's mind raced.

"They must be going back to Benton. I've got to get back there as well and find out who the Colonel is. He's got to be the key to this whole operation. And I've got to do it before that riverboat, the *Minerva Belle*, starts on its way back down the Missouri.

134

"Perhaps it's already left," MacGregor murmured.

"No . . . they usually stay a few days. That Colonel or whatever he is must be waiting for something, just like this gang is waiting. O'Shaughnessy brought them something from the unknown man on the *Minerva Belle*, a message or orders. Now he's going back to that man. Something's brewing, and I've got to find out what it is."

"And hoo do ye reckon ye'll do that?"

"Dutch Schultz! If I can find out who the Colonel is and then get Schultz up here to identify some of that gang, we'll have the start of something that we can turn over to the United States Army."

MacGregor rubbed his big chin. "Contrary tae what I thought when I first met ye, I'm noo thinkin' ye'll make a verra guid policeman—*if* ye dinna get your bluidy head shot off first."

Cavannagh slapped the brawny Scot on the shoulder. "Come on, let's sneak back up through these rocks and get out of here. Then while I'm rounding up Schultz and trying to find out who the big boss on the *Minerva Belle* is, I want you and Jenkins to watch that cleft from cover over behind the hill where we were this morning. It's the only way into and out of this camp, other than over the top like this, and they sure as hell won't be riding their horses up here."

Sergeant MacGregor grinned, and together they snaked their way back through the rocks to the edge of the outcropping and down to Jenkins on the outside.

135

A shrill whistle blasted the prairie morning stillness as the *Fontanna*'s blunt prow nosed through the muddy brown water of the Missouri. Two horsemen sat their saddles on the riverbank and watched the one hundred and thirty foot stern-wheeler thresh its way around the bend.

When the vessel drew closer, one of the horsemen stood in his stirrups and waved. A moment later the paddle steamer veered toward the bank. The captain stepped out of the wheelhouse and leaned over the top deck railing. Cupping his hands around his mouth, he shouted.

"Hello, there. What do you want?"

The tall blond horseman shouted back. "I have an important letter for the captain."

The captain turned and motioned to the pilot. The pilot craned his neck, studied the water, then instructed the wheelman to move the *Fontanna* closer to the bank.

"You might have to get your boots wet, mister," the captain shouted as the stern-wheeler got closer, then swung straight ahead again. "We're loaded pretty full and drawin' a bit more water than normal."

The two horsemen pushed their horses into the river, until the muddy brown water swirled above the horses' knees. The stern-wheeler slowed and the captain descended the narrow, nearly vertical stairway to the main deck.

The blond horseman turned in his saddle to speak to the buckskin-clad half-breed beside him. "You know what to do, Prefontaine."

"*Oui*, Mr. Fraser," the *Metis* nodded, giving a

heavy emphasis to the *mister*.

As the *Fontanna*'s deck came sliding by, Mr. Fraser lifted his saddlebags, swung his leg over the horse, and landed lightly aboard. When the captain stepped forward, the young blond man reached into the inside pocket of his gray coat, withdrew a long white envelope, and handed it to him.

The *Metis* reached for the riderless horse's reins, turned around in two and a half feet of brown water, and splashed back to shore.

Giving two blasts of her whistle, the *Fontanna* swung back toward midstream, picked up a little speed, and continued on her creaking, threshing way westward.

Chapter 12

Cavannagh walked his horse down the hill, watching the line shack on the opposite slope and waiting tensely for a bullet to fly past his head. When it didn't come as he got closer, he began to fear that Dutch Schultz had pulled out, but then he glimpsed Schultz's roan in the corral at the back. His next thought was that the Colonel's gunmen had got to him, and Cavannagh half expected to reach the shack and find Schultz's bullet-riddled body lying on the floor.

The door opened and a man appeared in the shadow.

"You must have been sleeping on the job, Dutch," Cavannagh called to him across thirty yards of grassed slope.

A chuckle emanated from the man in the doorway. "Naw. I saw you the minute your head topped that rise. I figgered you'd be back."

That statement surprised Cavannagh. "Oh — why?"

Schultz stepped out into the light of day. "I'm gettin' to know you better all the time, Lieutenant.

138

You just never could leave things well enough be. Typical West Point."

Cavannagh reined to in front of Schultz. He looked better than he had the last time. His clothes were clean and he had shaved and obviously bathed. He must have guessed what was going through Cavannagh's mind, for he chuckled again. "Got caught in the rain."

His face had lost the puffiness, too. He looked more like the Dutch Schultz whom Cavannagh used to know.

Cavannagh stared down at him from his saddle. "Aren't you going to invite me to stay awhile?"

Schultz grinned and squinted up at him, raising his hand to shade his eyes from the bright morning sun. "What for? You're just gonna want to ride out again. That's what you're here for. You ain't got very far in your investigation, and now you want me to help you. Ain't that right?"

Cavannagh decided not to wait any longer for an invitation, so he kicked his leg out of the stirrup, swung it over his horse's back, and climbed down out of the saddle.

"You're partly right, but I picked up some information in Benton that you might be interested in."

Schultz spat a brown stream of tobacco juice onto the autumn-dried grass. "I'm listenin'."

An appetizing aroma drifted out through the line shack's door.

"You could offer me a cup of coffee."

Schultz inclined his head and went back into the shack. Cavannagh unsaddled his horse and followed him. When he stepped into the shack, Shultz was sitting at the table with a tin cup of steaming black coffee. Another cup was on the table in front of a second chair. Cavannagh pushed his hat back off his head, sat down, lifted his cup, and sipped. The strong black liquid scalded his lips. Schultz grinned over the top of his cup.

"Have you gone off Montana red-eye?"

Schultz put down his cup. "I run out," he said simply. "What was it you had to tell me?"

Cavannagh told him about the conversation he had overheard in the livery stable at Fort Benton. Schultz listened, and when Cavannagh finished, the Civil War veteran sat in silence, staring past the younger man. His blue eyes had turned ice cold.

Finally, Schultz said, "Funny thing . . . I've been thinking since the other time you were out here that there's no percentage in me just sittin' holed up like this. With winter comin', I was goin' to hit out anyway. Only now it's goin' to be east to Benton instead of southwest to California."

With that, he pushed his chair back, stood up, and stepped over to the bunk. He rolled his blankets into a groundsheet-covered bedroll and strapped it. Next, he tossed a few things—shaving gear, clothing, matches, dried food, tobacco, two boxes of .44-40 rifle shells—into his saddlebags and checked his gun belt to make sure all the bullet loops were filled. After that, he drew both his six-guns and tested the actions and chambers, then thrust them back into their holsters. Finally he reached up to a leather jacket hanging from a nail on the wall and put it on, jammed a battered, wide-brimmed hat onto his head, and picked up his Winchester.

A wicked gleam in his ice-blue eyes, Dutch Schultz looked at Cavannagh and said, "Let's go."

They rode together across the rolling prairie, heading east, then northeast, then east again, toward Fort Benton. For a long time neither man spoke.

Then Cavannagh broke the silence.

"You seem pretty burned up over this."

"You're goddamned right I'm burned up. Them sons of bitches — tryin' to feed me to a Sioux scalping party!"

"What do you intend doing?"

"I'm goin' into Benton and hunt down that half-Crow bastard Johnny Buffalo and hammer him full of forty-fours. Then I'm gonna do the same to Meldrum if he happens to be around. After that I'll shoot any other son of a bitch who looks at me wrong-like." He paused for breath before adding, "That'll be for starters. But most of all I want to find out who that goddamned so-called partner of mine was, Colonel or whatever. I want him more'n I want that stinkin' half-Crow."

Jogging along beside Schultz, Cavannagh said, "You're too burned up to do the job properly. Why don't you cool down and combine your efforts with mine?"

Schultz mulled that over as they rode. After another mile he answered.

"Yeah . . . I guess mebbe you're right. You got a plan?"

"Slow down and I'll tell you what I've found out."

They reined their horses to a walk and Cavannagh told Schultz about following O'Shaughnessy, Meldrum, and Buffalo Johnny to the *Minerva Belle,* and then to the mysterious camp among the rock mass on the other side of the Marias. Schultz listened in silence until Cavannagh finished, then let forth.

"That big bald-headed son of a bitch you described — that's Egg-Head Vinsett. He's crazier than a rabid prairie dog an' meaner'n a gut-shot grizzly. He was the go-between for me and my so-called former partner. If this suspicion of yours is right, he's doin' the job that should've gone to me. Yeah, Cavannagh . . . I'm beginnin' to see somethin' that don't please me none. Fact is, I'm gonna add Egg-Head to my list."

Cavannagh cast a sideways glance at Schultz. "He looks as though he'd be a pretty mean opponent."

Schultz snorted. "Hell! I can take him. I can draw a six-gun faster than he can pull that Dakota scalping knife he carries instead of a handgun. Goddamn him — that's proof he's crazy. Any white man who carries a Sioux scalping knife instead of a six-gun . . ." Schultz shook his head in wonderment. "The way things are with the Sioux, sentiment runnin' the way it is, I'm surprised some white man hasn't laced him full of lead already."

Cavannagh nodded soberly. "I know what you mean. The man must have some strange twist of mind. I'll remember that if I have to deal with him."

"You let me deal with him. I reckon I got a score to settle there."

This sort of talk made Cavannagh realize that he was on the verge of getting more involved in this business than Major Walsh would approve. He didn't want to disobey the major's orders, but right now he was betwixt and between. He had to go on because he didn't yet have enough information to pass on to the U.S. Army. However, now that he had Dutch Schultz's help, he might soon find out what he needed to know, he reflected.

But he had to keep Dutch's burning urge for revenge channeled in the right direction. It could destroy everything and land him in a pile of trouble, threatening his new career in the North West Mounted Police. Through rashness and impropriety he had ruined his army career, and he had no desire to jeopardize another.

The main thing was to convince Schultz that by helping him to unravel this army-raiding operation and to discover the identity of the elusive Colonel, Dutch would be gaining the revenge he sought, even if not directly by his own hand.

The sun had been down for more than an hour when they rode into Benton, and splashes of yellow light from the saloons, gambling dens, billiard parlors, and dance halls lit up the darkened main street. Shouts, laughter, tinny music, and other sounds of revelry filled the evening air.

They stabled their horses, then walked down to the riverboat landing. There were two vessels docked. To Cavannagh's relief, the *Minerva Belle* was one of them. A few lights shone here and there from her decks and windows, but otherwise she looked nearly deserted.

"Ever been on a riverboat?" Cavannagh asked.

"A couple of times."

They walked up the gangway and stepped onto the

deck. Despite the stillness and deserted appearance of the stern-wheeler, Cavannagh half expected several burly Negro deckhands to suddenly materialize. They walked along the deck, the high heels of their riding boots making a distinctive *click-clack* on the hard wood, their spur rowels jingling musically. Cavannagh paused, about to bend down and take off his spurs, when Schultz, following behind, grimaced and suddenly doubled up. Cavannagh caught the movement.

"What's the matter, Dutch?"

Schultz grunted a couple of times and straightened up. "Nothin'. Just a passing gut pain."

Cavannagh frowned. "Are you all right?"

Schultz nodded. "Yeah . . . let's keep goin'."

Cavannagh mounted the stairway and climbed to the upper deck. Again he expected burly deckhands to come sauntering around the corner, but he and Schultz had the deck to themselves.

"They turned in here," Cavannagh said when he came to the entranceway through which he saw O'Shaughnessy and his two companions disappear that night.

"That leads to the passenger cabins," Schultz told him.

Cavannagh stepped through the entranceway into a lighted passageway that led across to the other side of the deck, with another lighted passageway branching off at right angles. He turned down this, Schultz following, and walked its length. There were numbered doors on each side.

"This is one of the fancier paddle steamers," Schultz said. "Mostly the cabins open from the deck.

Leastwise, the ones I seen did."

They retraced their steps along the passageway and returned to the deck.

"Well, what now?" Schultz asked.

Cavannagh rubbed his jaw. "There must be a passenger register somewhere aboard. I'd like to get my hands on it."

"We could go lookin' for it. I'm kinda anxious to find out who this Colonel dude is. My trigger finger's gettin' itchy."

They were about to further explore the stern-wheeler when the sound of voices from the street beyond the landing distracted them. The voices were getting closer. Two shadowy figures moved through the gloom toward the landing. Presently the figures emerged into the dull orange light thrown from two lanterns on the dock. At the same instant, Cavannagh recognized O'Shaughnessy's voice. He pushed Schultz and himself out of sight against the wall.

Still talking, O'Shaughnessy and the other man stepped onto the gangway and alighted onto the deck. Their footsteps sounded across the deck and up the stairway, but before their heads came level with the upper deck, Cavannagh and Schultz disappeared down the passageway. When O'Shaughnessy and his companion turned into the passageway, Cavannagh and Schultz were again out of sight, this time on the far side of the deck.

The Irishman and his associate turned right and walked along the passageway where they stopped while O'Shaughnessy's companion dug his hand into his coat pocket and produced a key. He inserted it into the lock, opened a cabin door, and stepped inside, O'Shaughnessy following. The door closed behind them as Cavannagh's head peered around the corner, just in time to see which cabin they'd entered.

Cavannagh motioned to Schultz and together they tiptoed along the passageway to the cabin into which the two men had disappeared. Cavannagh pressed his ear to the door. He could hear two voices, one of which was O'Shaughnessy's.

"Who are those two dudes?" Schultz whispered.

"O'Shaughnessy," Cavannagh whispered back. "I didn't get a good look at the other one, except to see he's wearing a black suit. But my guess is he's the Colonel."

"Then let's kick the door in. Like I told you, my trigger finger's getting' itchy."

"No! I've got to find out a few things first." Cavannagh held a finger to his mouth. "Shh! I'm trying to hear what they're saying."

After listening for a few minutes, Cavannagh felt a hand tap his shoulder. Impatiently he turned his head.

"We can't stand here all damned night," Schultz whispered.

"You're right. Try the next cabin."

Schultz crept along the passageway to the next cabin and tried the door. It opened and he went inside. A moment later he stuck his head out and nodded. Cavannagh joined him inside and shut the door. Schultz struck a match and held the flame up. The cabin was empty and showed no signs of occupancy.

"You can hear real good against this wall," Schultz whispered, indicating the wall between the two

146

cabins.

Cavannagh moved over to the wall and pressed his ear against it. He could hear the same two voices. His pulse beat quickly as excitement gripped him.

Chapter 13

Ear pressed to the stateroom wall, Cavannagh listened intently, scarcely daring to breathe lest he miss some of the conversation taking place on the other side.

"For our plans to succeed," he heard an older man's voice say, "it's essential that you wipe out the Mounted Police at Fort Walsh and Fort Macleod just before winter. By the time the Canadian government finds out, it'll be too late for them to act. They won't be able to move reinforcements across the prairies before next summer. By then Sitting Bull will have the entire Missouri River country in flames. With no redcoats along the international boundary to stop them, the Blackfoot and Crees won't be able to resist the temptation to join in. That will create the right climate for our lobbyists in Washington to urge the United States government to move up and annex everything north of the forty-ninth parallel between Manitoba and the Rocky Mountains."

"And what do oi get out of it for takin' all the risks, Colonel?" O'Shaughnessy's voice was unmistakable.

"Riches beyond your wildest dreams, Michael. Do

you realize the potential of that vast, resource-rich country all the way up to the Arctic Ocean, bounded only by Hudson Bay to the east and Alaska to the west? Man, there's a fortune in furs alone! Don't forget, I represent a group of wealthy and powerful businessmen and politicians in both the United States and Canada who have a vested interest in seeing Ottawa abandon the North West Territories. I have the influence to secure for you the directorship of a company with sole fur-trading rights throughout the north. That will provide you with the finances to help your Fenian friends carry on their fight to drive the British out of Ireland."

"And what do you aspire to, Colonel?"

"The governorship of one of the new territories."

So intently was Cavannagh listening that he jumped when Dutch Schultz tapped him on the shoulder.

"I got the damnedest fire in my bowels that you'd ever imagine," Dutch whispered. "I gotta find me a place to drop what's burnin' 'em."

Impatiently Cavannagh whispered back. "Go ahead, but don't be long."

Cavannagh turned his attention back to the conversation in the adjoining stateroom. He was conscious of a shaft of light briefly falling across the floor behind him as Schultz opened the door and stepped out into the passageway.

O'Shaughnessy was talking again. "How do oi know you won't double-cross me like you did Dutch Schultz?"

The older man's voice laughed. "Double-cross is a harsh word, Michael. Schultz couldn't take orders. If he'd got to that rendezvous with Crooked Moon's Sioux when he was supposed to, what we're now trying to accomplish would have been done."

"But you'd already arranged with Crooked Moon to kill Schultz when he got the rifles instead of giving him gold. That was before you knew he hadn't followed your orders."

The older man laughed again. "Schultz was too ambitious, Michael. Egg-Head warned me about him. It would've been only a matter of time before he tried to take over, but I don't have to worry about you. You don't give a tinker's damn about American politics. You burn with hate for the British because they chased you out of your country. You live for the day when you can go back, smote them with your double-edged sword, and run up the shamrock flag over your native isle."

Cavannagh didn't notice the door open behind him, and it wasn't until a shaft of light from the passageway beamed across the floor that he realized someone had entered the room. Then he heard a heavy footsteps on the floor.

"Freeze, mister!"

Cavannagh froze. He recognized the voice—it wasn't Dutch Schultz!

"Git your hands up an' move over a little more into the light. I want to git a good look at yew."

Cavannagh raised his arms and rose from his bending position. Stiff from kneeling, he momentarily lost his balance and thudded against the wall.

"No tricks," the voice warned sharply. "Move over into the light like I told yew. That's right. Now turn around slow-like."

150

Cavannagh turned around to find himself staring into the blue barrel of a Remington .44 held in the hand of William Meldrum.

Meldrum grinned. "Well . . . I'll be damned! Corporal Cavannagh of the North West Mounted. I told yew up in Canada that if yew ever returned to Montana, I'd kill yew."

Meldrum pulled back the .44's hammer. "An' thet's just what I'm goin' to do right now."

Cavannagh turned ice cold.

But it was O'Shaughnessy's voice that stayed Meldrum's trigger finger.

"What the divil's going on in here?"

"If'n yew want to light one of them lamps," Meldrum said over his shoulder to the Irishman standing in the doorway behind him, "yew'll find yoreself with a mighty unwelcome surprise."

O'Shaughnessy stepped into the cabin and put a match to one of the cabin lamps. Turning it up full, he peered intently at Cavannagh but didn't speak until Meldrum reached forward and flicked Cavannagh's hat brim, flipping the hat back off his head. O'Shaughnessy's hazel eyes widened with recognition.

"What the divil are you doing here?"

It was Meldrum who answered. "I caught him with his ear agin' thet wall listenin' to whatever yew an' the Colonel was talkin' about."

O'Shaughnessy's red eyebrows arched. "How mooch did you hear?"

Cavannagh looked back at him defiantly. "Enough."

Meldrum waved his .44 menacingly. "It won't do him no good. I'll jes' put a bullet into him."

151

O'Shaugnessy held up his hand. "Wait!" Then he stared at Cavannagh. "How did you foind us here? You couldn't have followed us from Fort Walsh . . ."

Cavannagh couldn't help a smile tugging the corners of his mouth.

"Yew got one hell of a sense of humor for a man who's about to die, Cavannagh," Meldrum interjected.

"You won't find the Mounted Police easy to wipe out," Cavannagh said to the Irishman. "They might be new to the West and there's not that many of them, but they're well trained and well disciplined."

O'Shaughnessy's yellow teeth showed against his red beard. "Single-shot Snider carbines won't stand mooch chance against Winchester repeaters. Besides—"

Whatever else the Irishman was about to say was abruptly cut short by a sharp voice barking out from the passageway behind him. "Michael!"

O'Shaughnessy turned. Cavannagh could see the shoulder of a small man wearing a black coat just around the corner of the door. The Irishman stepped out of the cabin after a quick word to Meldrum to watch Cavannagh. He stood just around the corner in the passageway for a minute or two, conversing with the man in the black coat. Cavannagh craned his neck to see more, but Meldrum waved the .44 under his nose.

"It won't do yew no good, yew British-lovin' son of a bitch! Yew've come to the end of yore trail."

A moment later O'Shaughnessy stepped back into the cabin. "Toi Cavannagh oop," he said to Meldrum. *"Tie him up?"*

"That's what oi said."

"Hell! I'll put a bullet into him. He knows too much."

"Oi said toi him oop!" O'Shaughnessy snapped. "A bullet makes too mooch noise. The sheriff in this town seems to have a habit of being drawn by the sound of shots, and undue attention is the last thing we want roight now."

Grumbling, Meldrum handed the Irishman his .44 and rummaged through a pair of saddlebags half-hidden in a corner of the cabin. Producing a length of rope, he grabbed Cavannagh's upstretched arms and roughly tied them behind his back. Then he kicked Cavannagh's feet from under him, sending him dropping heavily to the floor, and ran the rope around each ankle, pulling his legs up behind him so that he couldn't move. Finally he removed Cavannagh's gun belt and stood looking down maliciously at the younger man.

"Well, he won't get out of that."

Watching, O'Shaughnessy said, "Now gag him."

Meldrum glanced around the cabin, reached for a hand towel, leaned over Cavannagh, and stuffed it into his mouth. Then he tied it into place with Cavannagh's cavalry-yellow bandanna.

"Good," O'Shaughnessy smirked, handing the .44 back to Meldrum.

"Now what?" Meldrum asked.

Grinning with satisfaction, O'Shaughnessy said, "This boat will be leavin' soon. When she's well on her way, at some isolated spot along the Missouri, we'll doomp him over the side."

O'Shaughnessy stepped to the door. "Now we'll just

turn out the loight and lock the cabin. We'll slip a dollar or two to one of them big black deckhands to stand guard in the passageway to make sure no one gets in here, just in case Corporal Cavannagh has any friends around."

Mr. Fraser stood at the upper-deck railing and watched the muddy brown water slide sluggishly by as the *Fontanna* threshed her tortuous way around bend after bend of the winding Missouri. He was terribly bored.

In an effort to shake the boredom, he pushed himself away from the railing, climbed the stairway to the top deck, and made his way to the wheelhouse. The captain met him at the door.

"Afraid I've some bad news, Mr. Fraser."

The expression of boredom on the blond young man's face was replaced by one of concern. "Oh?"

The captain cleared his throat. "Water's running a bit low. Lot of sandbars, more than usual at this time of year. Seeing as how we're heavily loaded, we might have trouble getting all the way to Benton. And we don't want to get caught on the river if an early winter sets in. It's getting on in—"

Mr. Fraser cut in impatiently. "Precisely what does that mean, Captain?"

The captain cleared his throat again. "Well . . . we'll probably pull in to Cow Island, unload all our freight ashore, then turn around and head back to St. Louis."

"Cow Island? How far is that from Fort Benton?"

"About sixty miles. But you don't have to worry.

When we don't turn up in Benton on schedule, the I.G. Baker Company sends a bull train along to Cow Island to pick up the freight. You might get a little lonely for two or three days, but there's no need to worry."

But Mr. Fraser did worry.

Chapter 14

Dutch Schultz felt naked without his guns. For the twentieth time he wondered where they were.

After he had left Cavannagh, he had searched half the riverboat before finding a toilet. But finding one at last, he had gone in, hung his gun belt on a hook on the wall, and entered a tight little cubicle, where he had dropped his pants and sat down on the wooden toilet seat. While he had been seated, someone had entered the washroom, used the facilities, and left. But when Schultz had finished evacuating his bowels and stepped out of the cubicle, his gun belt was gone. Despite a frantic search up and down the passageway, he didn't find his guns.

When he had made his way back to join Cavannagh, he had noticed the tempo picking up on the *Minerva Belle*. Passengers were now boarding and cargo was being loaded onto the top deck. When he had reached the stateroom in which he had left Cavannagh, Dutch found a big, muscular Negro deckhand guarding the door and he had barely managed to duck back around the passageway corner without being seen.

Now the damned stern-wheeler was threshing its

boat back into the main stream.

He watched with foreboding as a thick column of smoke belched from her high black funnel and she swung around eastward and headed back down the Missouri. Beside him were rows of heavily nailed wooden cases, each case measuring three feet long, two feet wide, and eighteen inches high. Each case was marked in black paint: *Merchandise — Canadian Government.*

It was incredible. Here he was, isolated and alone, with one hundred wooden cases, which any fool could see were ammunition boxes. He cursed the criminal stupidity of the Ottawa official who had initiated the dispatch of this valuable and vital shipment across hundreds of miles of hostile country infested with drifting outlaws and warlike Indians, without adequate protection at a time when armed parties of soldiers were escorting similar American shipments across these dangerous Missouri plains.

Grim faced, Mr. Fraser stood at the water's edge watching the *Fontanna*'s paddle-driven stern grow smaller and smaller as his own sense of isolation grew larger and larger.

Chapter 15

Every sense alert, Dutch Schultz crept stealthily along the dimly lit passageway between the upper-deck cabins. But he saw nothing and heard nothing, save for the threshing of the *Minerva Belle*'s stern wheel and the groaning of her timbers. His palms sweated, despite the cool of the night, and the blood pounded steadily in his temples.

He guessed the time to be about three A.M.

The Colonel's stateroom was just around the corner. Dutch pressed his back against the wall, reached around to a bowie knife at his belt, and slowly peered around the corner. The big Negro deckhand was gone from in front of the cabin in which Cavannagh was a prisoner. Good!

Schultz stepped around the corner and tiptoed down the passageway. Reaching the cabin, he looked around quickly and tried the door. It was locked.

He inserted the bowie's blade into the space between the lock and doorjamb and tried to work the lock loose. It resisted his efforts. For a moment he wrestled with the temptation to kick the door in, then resumed working with the knife. Beads of sweat popped out on his brow, as the thought crossed his mind that the big Negro might be inside waiting.

Damn it all! What he'd give to have his two equalizers belted around his waist right now.

After what seemed like an eternity he could feel the lock giving. He worked at it with renewed effort until half a minute later it opened. With poised knife he sprang inside, expecting to be jumped. But only Cavannagh was in the dark room, lying bound and gagged on the floor.

Shutting the door behind him, Dutch lit a lamp, bent down over Cavannagh, and cut the rope around his ankles and wrists. Then he pulled the gag from Cavannagh's mouth.

Cavannagh gazed up at him through lidded eyes. "Water," he croaked hoarsely. Dutch gave him water from a pitcher.

"You're in a bad way," Dutch said, noting the haggard look on Cavannagh's unshaven face and the rope burns around his wrists. "What the hell happened?"

It took Cavannagh several seconds before he could speak, and he did so in a hoarse whisper. "Meldrum . . . got the . . . drop on me."

"Too bad I got that gut ache. Anyways, we gotta get out of here. That big black man might come back."

As Cavannagh struggled to get to his feet, Dutch suggested, "Take it easy. You've been tied a long time. Better get your circulation back."

Cavannagh rested, letting his blood circulate freely, massaging the stiffness out of his legs and arms.

"Where are O'Shaughnessy and the Colonel?"

"O'Shaughnessy left the boat yesterday," Schultz

161

whispered. "The Colonel's still aboard near as I can reckon. Come on, see if you can walk now."

This time Cavannagh was able to stand and walk haltingly to the door. Schultz helped him along the passageway toward the stairway to the top deck. He could feel Cavannagh's strength returning as they climbed the stairway. "You're doin' fine . . . just a little ways further."

At the top of the stairway Dutch warned, "We got to be careful here. The wheelhouse is just over there. Keep low."

Under a myriad of bright stars sprinkled against the night sky's velvet blackness, they stole across the top deck behind the wheelhouse until they gained the sanctuary of the cargo. Dutch guided Cavannagh in under the smelly buffalo hides.

Rummaging around, Dutch found a cloth sack, which he had cached earlier, and handed it to Cavannagh. "I went foraging around the kitchen and rustled up some grub. There's bread and chicken, even a little fruit." He turned to go.

Cavannagh gripped his arm. "Where are you going?"

"I got something to do. You stay here until I get back."

Schultz crept back across the deck, moving around the cargo, along behind the wheelhouse, keeping well into the shadows cast by the big light in front of the wheelhouse that lit up the river ahead, and slunk down the stairs to the passageway. Again the blood pounded in his temples as he contemplated his next move. He held his bowie knife in front of him, still wishing he had his six-guns.

162

Reaching the corner leading to the Colonel's state-room, Schultz again cautiously peered around it. Everything appeared normal. The big Negro deck-hand must have been so confident that Cavannagh couldn't escape that he had gone to bed instead of standing guard. Schultz grinned, slipped around the corner, and moved along the passageway.

Outside the Colonel's door, he knocked softly. Hearing no answer, he knocked again, a little harder, and called through the door in a low tone.

"Colonel, open up. It's Meldrum. I got something to tell you."

Two or three seconds later he heard movement in the stateroom. "What was that?" a voice answered thickly from behind the door.

"It's Meldrum, Colonel," Schultz lied. "Open up. I got to see you. Something went wrong."

There was the sound of the door being unlocked. Dutch tensed himself and as soon as it opened a crack he threw his hip and shoulder at it and it flew open.

A startled, florid-faced little man with sleep-di-sheveled gray hair and a flowing gray moustache staggered back. Schultz kicked shut the door behind him and grabbed the little man by his nightshirt collar.

"So you're the Colonel, huh?" Dutch grated, ram-ming him against the wall. "You're the big boss-man, my former partner?"

"Who are you?" the Colonel managed to splutter.

"Ernest Schultz, but they call me Dutch. Dutch Schultz . . . "you remember? I'm the hombre you arranged with the Sioux to kill up in Canadian territory, you double-crossin' son of a bitch!"

163

The Colonel's eyes bulged. He grabbed Dutch's wrist with both hands. "You're choking me, damn it!"

"Chokin' you—you little son of a bitch! I'm goin' to kill you. No man's goin' to arrange with no goddamned Indians to kill me, then when that don't work spread the word that I double-crossed him, and then send guns out to get me. Leastwise, no man's goin' to do that and live to talk about it."

The florid color drained from the Colonel's face until it was a deathly white. "Now wait a minute . . . I can explain . . . I'll make everything right . . ."

"No you won't, you murderin' little bastard. *I'm* goin' to set it right."

With a sudden lunge, Dutch thrust the bowie knife into the Colonel's belly immediately below the rib cage, then jerked upward. The Colonel's face showed incredulity, his eyes popped, and a stream of blood trickled down his mouth. Schultz released his hold on the Colonel's nightshirt and the scheming little gray-haired man slid down the stateroom wall to the floor.

Schultz quickly looked around the stateroom, locked his eyes on to a chest of drawers, and pulled them open. In one he found what he wanted—a Smith & Wesson .44. He snatched it up and checked the chambers. Loaded. Shoving it into his belt, he rummaged around until he found a box of shells, which he emptied into his pockets. Then he turned out the lamp and left the stateroom.

A few minutes later he was back with Cavannagh among the buffalo skins. "We gotta get off'n this thing pronto," he said just loud enough to be heard over the threshing sound of the paddle wheel.

"I can't leave," Cavannagh replied. "The Colonel—"

"Don't worry about him," Schultz interrupted. "He's gone too. Come on, we ain't got time to waste."

They sneaked out from under the smelly bales, crossed the top deck behind the wheelhouse, and hurried down the stairway to the passageway below, following it until they were out on the upper passenger deck. They stayed in the shadows until they were sure there were no crewmen around, then darted along to the stairway leading to the lower deck. Seconds later they were down by the railing, just a foot above the passing water.

Before throwing his leg over the rail, Schultz grabbed at Cavannagh. "You ready for a swim?"

"I don't have much choice."

Schultz swung himself over the rail and dropped into the water, driving out with strong strokes for the shore. The cold water shocked his system and he swam vigorously. It had the same effect on Cavannagh, for he was right behind Schultz.

The *Minerva Belle*'s lights glided quickly away from them. By the time they staggered up the river's bank, the lights had disappeared around a bend.

Dawn found them squishing along the Missouri's north bank—cold, wet, and hungry. Schultz carried some waterproof matches, but in the dark they hadn't been able to find any fuel. Now in daylight they could see lots of buffalo chips on the prairie, but they wondered whether it was wise to light a fire. The smoke would be seen a long way, there might be hostile Indians around, and they only had the one gun and two pockets of shells between them.

"It boils down to a choice between hostiles or pneumonia," Schultz asked.

"I don't want to take the time," Cavannagh said without breaking his stride. "We've got a long way to go."

Schultz snorted. "Hell! You don't even know where the blue blazes you're goin'. You just set your head down like a buffalo bull and charge. I reckon they must've had fun with you at West Point."

Cavannagh threw renewed energy into his stride. "We're wasting time."

Schultz shook his head in submission and followed Cavannagh's footsteps.

But after another hour Schultz had his way and they hunkered down over a fire of dried grass and buffalo chips, drying their wet clothes and boots piece by piece. Schultz lay out the Smith & Wesson and the .44 shells near the fire, hoping to dry the black powder sufficiently to make the weapon and bullets usable.

"This has got to be the plumb stupidest thing I ever heard of," Schultz complained. "Two of us out here in the middle of nowhere, on foot, without guns, no food . . . without even knowin' where we're goin'."

Cavannagh sat staring into the fire.

"If'n I had half a brain, I wouldn't have ever throwd in with you. You've got me into some damn tight places."

Cavannagh didn't take his eyes from the glowing buffalo chips as he answered. "You got yourself into them, Dutch. If you hadn't broken Canadian law and run afoul of the Mounted Police, none of this would have happened."

Schultz chuckled. "No . . . I guess not."

Cavannagh reached over to his pants stretched out on some rocks he'd found by the river. While pulling them on, he suddenly froze, his eyes on the horizon to the northeast.

Schultz noticed Cavannagh's strange stance and followed the direction of his stare. Immediately he saw it—a cloud of dust coming over the prairie. The same question filled both their minds—hostiles or friends?—but neither voiced it.

Cavannagh pulled on his boots. Schultz reached for the Smith & Wesson and quickly pushed shells into the chambers. Cavannagh picked up a couple of rocks.

The dust rolled closer, the cloud now widening as though the horses and riders making it were spreading out.

Indians!

But it was a column of bluecoats that trotted over the rolling hills, spreading out into a flanking line. Obviously they were taking no chances until they ascertained the cause of the smoke.

Seeing two lone white men, the officer in charge shouted an order and hand signaled the soldiers back into columns of twos. Dutch Schultz stuck his revolver back into his belt as the cavalry approached. Cavannagh stood motionless, seized by a poignant sense of loss as he watched the familiar blue uniforms coming closer and listened to the clink of bridles, the creak of saddle leather.

The soldiers reined to a halt in front of them—a

lieutenant, a sergeant, two corporals, twenty men, and six pack horses. The single gold bars on the lieutenant's oblong shoulder tabs were faded and his face bore the strain of years of service.

"Good morning," the lieutenant said, taking in Cavannagh's cavalry pants and boots. From Cavannagh the officer's eyes flickered to Schultz, but remained there for only an instant before returning to Cavannagh. Cavannagh saw the questions in the lieutenant's eyes.

"My name is Cavannagh, Lieutenant . . . late of the Seventh Cavalry." He inclined his head to Schultz. "This is my companion, Mr. Schultz."

The lieutenant grunted. "The Seventh, eh . . . Custer's outfit. Right down to the buckskin jacket. Looks like you two ran into some sort of trouble."

"It's a long story, Lieutenant," Cavannagh replied. "It will take a while to tell."

The lieutenant eased forward in his saddle and looked down at Cavannagh. "Mister, when you've been a one-bar as long as I have, time doesn't matter much." He turned to the sergeant. "Dismount the patrol, Sergeant. We'll rest here a bit. Points out."

While the soldiers took a break, Cavannagh told the lieutenant that he was a member of the North West Mounted Police and gave him a summary of what had happened since he left Fort Walsh. Finishing with the sequence of events on the *Minerva Belle,* he explained that he and Schultz were walking back to Fort Benton.

The lieutenant said, "We're going there on our way back to Fort Shaw. We can take you with us, but we may have to stop at Cow Island first and guard any freight the riverboats might have dropped off." He motioned to the sergeant. "Redistribute the loads on the pack animals. These two gentlemen will accompany us. Then prepare the patrol to move out."

"Yessir."

Five minutes later Cavannagh and Schultz struck out westward with the cavalry patrol.

When the patrol rode down onto Cow Island an hour before sundown, a scene of humming activity met their eyes. A dozen or more ox-drawn Baker Company wagons stood while a hundred heavily nailed wooden cases marked *Merchandise—Canadian Government* were being loaded aboard. A wagon boss supervised, while a tall blond man and a man wearing a badge on his coat and carrying a sheaf of papers in his hand watched. The lieutenant halted his patrol and spoke to the man with the badge.

"I'm Lieutenant Caldwell from Fort Shaw. You must be Mr. Stevens, United States Customs at Fort Benton."

"That's right," the man with the badge nodded agreeably. Indicating the blond man with him, he added, "And this is Sub-Inspector Fraser of the North West Mounted Police at Fort Walsh."

Lieutenant Caldwell threw off a salute to Sub-Inspector Fraser, then swept his arm in the direction of the wooden cases being loaded aboard the wagons. "I take it that this is the shipment of Canadian merchandise."

Mr. Stevens nodded again. "That's right. Ammunition for the Mounted Police. Our government authorized its shipment through United States territory provided that a responsible Canadian officer accompanied it. I've given it customs clearance. It will all be loaded onto the wagons by sundown. The Baker bull train will start out northward with it at first light tomorrow."

"I see," the cavalry officer said. "Well, that simplifies my orders. I'll camp my men here for the night and accompany you to Fort Benton in the morning, Mr. Stevens." He turned around in his saddle and said to his sergeant, "Dismount the patrol, Sergeant. Pickets as usual."

Climbing down off his horse, Lieutenant Caldwell said to Sub-Inspector Fraser, "We picked up one of your men, Sub-Inspector. Corporal Cavannagh. A little worse for wear, I might add."

Sub-Inspector Fraser hadn't noticed Cavannagh, who had already dismounted and was walking forward, because Cavannagh and Schultz had been riding at the rear of the patrol. Cavannagh stopped in front of him.

"Good evening, sir."

"Good evening, Corporal. I would have presumed you to be back at Fort Walsh by now." There was a tone of sarcasm in the sub-inspector's voice. Only his arrogant politeness kept him from saying what he really meant: *What the hell are you doing here?*

"Your corporal has had some interesting adventures, Sub-Inspector," Lieutenant Caldwell said. "He has a story to tell."

Sub-Inspector Fraser turned to the cavalry officer. "I'm sure he has, *Leftenant*. He is an accomplished talker. I'll look forward to hearing it over supper."

They sat eating supper around three separate camp-fires—the Baker men around one, the soldiers around another, and Cavannagh, Schultz, Sub-Inspector Fraser, the customs officer, and Lieutenant Caldwell around the third. Cavannagh had just finished his story when one of the army sentries brought into camp two horsemen, each leading a saddled but riderless horse. Cavannagh sprang to his feet as the light from the fires illuminated them.

"Mac! Jenkins!"

Sergeant MacGregor was equally surprised. "Cavannagh! I'll be damned! So this is where ye are. I looked all over Fort Benton for ye. Then I noticed that that riverboat was gone, so I assumed ye must have boarded her. I found oot where ye and ye're friend Schultz had stabled ye're horses, so I brought 'em along."

"What happened to that band of raiders?"

MacGregor jerked a thumb over his shoulder. "They pulled oot of their lair as soon as they spotted this bull train. This must hae been what they've been waiting for. They followed it here, watched some stuff being loaded in the wagons, and struck on north for a bit. They've made camp five or six miles up. Is this bull train bound for north of the border?"

A voice from the fire answered. "Yes, Sergeant—Fort Walsh."

Sergeant MacGregor recognized the speaker, who was rising to his feet on the far side of the campfire. "Mr. Fraser, sirr. I hardly expected tae see ye here, sirr."

171

"The past few hours have been full of surprises, Sergeant. Right from the unexpectedly early appearance of the Baker bull train, then Corporal Cavannagh, now you. But tell me, this band of raiders you're talking about, are they the same raiders Corporal Cavannagh has told me about?"

"Aye, they would be, sirr. Last night, when they camped, I was able t' sneak up on them in the dark and overhear something o' wha' they were talking about. They were too busy gambling and talking aboot wild women, but they did say something interesting. They plan tae hit a bull train after it crosses the border. They must mean this one."

Sub-Inspector Fraser nodded, a somber expression drawing his face, the shadows of the campfire making him look older than his twenty-seven years. "The wagons in this train contain the ammunition supplies we've been waiting for."

MacGregor frowned. "But would they want it tha' badly? It's for Snider-Enfields. It'll nae fit Winchesters."

"They must want it, obviously."

Cavannagh wondered aloud. "But why should they wait until after the bull train crosses the border?"

"Mebbe they're figgerin' like I would," Dutch Schultz chipped in. "Mounted Police patrols seldom number more than a dozen men, sometimes only two or three. U.S. Cavalry patrols, in the other hand, run anywhere from twenty to sixty, depending on what sort of trouble they're expecting from Indians. A gang the size of this one we're talkin' about could fight its way out of a run-in with redcoats. They'd have trouble doin' it with the army."

172

Lieutenant Caldwell said admiringly to Sergeant MacGregor, as one old soldier to another, "You would have been a good man to have had around during the war, Sergeant. Any man who can get that close to a body of armed men like that without them being aware of it . . ."

Sergeant MacGregor beamed appreciatively. "It was child's play, sirr. In Africa I once got up so close t' a tribe of Ashanti that I could almost hae reached oot and taken the verra food oot o' their mouths."

Lieutenant Caldwell laughed. "Speaking of food, Sergeant, if you and your man haven't eaten, you're most welcome to join us."

"Thenk ye, sirr. That's verra kind of ye."

At daybreak the Baker wagons were ready to roll. Sub-Inspector Fraser stood off to the side of the hearing of the train boss and discussed with Cavannagh, Sergeant MacGregor, and Lieutenant Caldwell courses of action they had contemplated during the night.

"I don't want the Baker teamsters knowing that the train might be attacked," Sub-Inspector Fraser said. "For one thing, they won't be able to prevent it. For another they won't be able to unwittingly tip off the raiders that we're aware of their plans. And perhaps most importantly, if they know about it beforehand, they might refuse to take the wagons at all. We can't afford that. I don't want to be bloody-minded about this, but the force needs this ammunition."

Lieutenant Caldwell said, "I wish I could be of some help, gentlemen. Unfortunately, I can do very little, other than ride north to where your sergeant said that band of horsemen is camped and check them. But unless I find U.S. Army property in their possession, there is nothing I can do."

Cavannagh replied, "I doubt you'd find anything, Lieutenant. Besides, it wouldn't accomplish anything. Those men are part of a clever conspiracy bent on eliminating the Mounted Police. We have to find out how they plan to do that and stop them."

Sergeant MacGregor said, "Then I take it we follow the plan Corporal Cavannagh suggested last night, sirr? We ride south with the cavalry until we're well oot of sight, in case those raiders are watching us noo. Then we detour around and tail them until they make their move."

Sub-Inspector Fraser nodded.

"And if they are watching," the big Scot continued, "they'll think Cavannagh, Schultz, Constable Jenkins, and myself rode in wi' the cavalry and noo we're riding on with them."

"Yes," agreed the sub-inspector. "I'll go with the bull train. They know I'm here. They'd become suspicious otherwise."

Lieutenant Caldwell climbed up into his saddle. "Good luck, gentlemen." Then he raised his arm high above his head and swept it frontward and down. "Patrol . . . *forward ho!*"

The blue-coated troopers filed by, their accoutrements jingling. Cavannagh, MacGregor, Schultz, Jenkins, and Customs Officer Stevens pulled themselves up into their saddles and swung in behind the soldiers.

Sub-Inspector Fraser turned and walked across the

alkaline prairie to the bull train. He spoke a few words to the train boss and climbed up onto the lead wagon.

The train boss cracked his whip and boomed from his tobacco-stained lips, "Wagons . . . *ro-olll*."

Chapter 16

The Baker bull train moved across the wide brown prairie landscape at a rate of fourteen or fifteen miles a day. Paralleling it four or five miles away for the first two days were thirty-five heavily armed horsemen. But on the third day they cut around behind it and rode so far eastward that Cavannagh, watching them through field glasses, for the first time entertained serious doubts that his reasoning of their intentions was correct.

Sergeant MacGregor, riding stirrup-to-stirrup beside Cavannagh as they followed, shared the younger man's doubts. But not Dutch Schultz.

"They'll swing north pretty soon. Then they'll head up to the Canadian border through one of them long ravines, move across that dry alkaline country south and east of the Cypress Hills. If I was you, Cavannagh, I'd veer straight north right now, keep on going through the night, get across the border, and climb up onto that grassy plateau—you know the one."

Cavannagh turned in his saddle to face Schultz, riding with Freddie Jenkins behind him. "Old-Man-on-his-Back . . . east of Battle Creek?"

Schultz, rising in his saddle with the movement of

his roan, nodded. "That'd be the one. You know how wide a sweep you'd have of the border from up there. Especially with them field glasses. That's how you caught me."

"You're right, Dutch. It's a bit risky, though . . . in case we've misjudged their plans."

"The whole damn thing's a risk. But you keep tailing 'em like this, you'll be runnin' a bigger risk. They're bad business and they're used to trouble. They're plumb liable to put points out to see they ain't bein' followed, even if they ain't expectin' it, just in case. That's what I'd do."

Cavannagh turned to face front. He called back over his shoulder. "I thought about that. We could stay far enough behind and follow their dust. They won't put a point that far out. I don't want to lose them in case they pull something different."

Schultz glanced up at the sky, leaden and low. "You mightn't see their dust much longer. It's gonna either rain or snow. Anyways, if you hang too far back, you'll lose 'em once they get into that heavy timber in the Cypress Hills. You better do like I said."

Freddie, riding beside Schultz, made no effort to conceal a smirk on his hard, lantern-jawed face. He was enjoying Cavannagh's quandary.

After a moment of consideration, Cavannagh said, "Looks like we make a *half-sections left wheel*."

Sergeant MacGregor's ruggedly handsome face creased into a grin at Cavannagh's usage of British cavalry drill terminology, and the four of them wheeled their horses and changed direction north.

By midafternoon the leaden bottom of the threatening sky fell out and drenched the prairie and everything on it in a heavy, sodden rain that turned to sleet at the approach of dusk, and to a blinding snowstorm after dark.

The four northbound horsemen lowered their heads into the upturned collars of their dripping slickers. Cavannagh, his hat lost aboard the *Minerva Belle*, wrapped one of his blankets around his head.

"We're goin' to have to find shelter," Schultz yelled into Cavannagh's ear as they hunched over their saddle and urged their horses to plod on.

Cavannagh didn't want to stop. He didn't want to lose the time, but he knew Schultz was right. They had to rest their horses and feed themselves. Worse, they stood a good chance of losing not only time but their way as well.

Schultz knew what was going through Cavannagh's mind. "They'll have to stop, too. This storm's hittin' them as well."

They found a shelter under a cutbank, which kept the wind from them, and they were able to munch pemmican and beef jerky. Then they dozed in miserable bouts of fitful sleep, even Cavanangh, whose mind was consumed by the urgency of their task.

The storm passed by midmorning and they dug themselves out of a foot of snow. But when they climbed from beneath the cutbank up onto the prairie and looked around, Cavannagh shook his head, first in confusion — for ahead of him rose a low, snow-blanketed mountain, while far behind him stretched a long range of jeweled rocky peaks — then in anger, as Dutch Schultz put into words what Cavannagh had realized.

"Son of a bitch! We got turned around in that storm. We've been headin' in the wrong damned direction."

Cavannagh swore a stream of oaths that even shook Dutch Schultz.

"I didn't know West Point taught officers and gentlemen words like that."

"This isn't funny, Dutch."

"I ain't laughin', goddamn it."

Cavannagh shouted impatiently. "Mac, Jenkins — let's get moving. We've got to make up for lost time."

"We'd better let the horses forage through this snow for pasturage first," Sergeant MacGregor told him. "It'll save us time in the long run."

It was another hour before they got going, putting the low mountains — the Bear Paws — where they should have been, over their right shoulders, and the far-off peaks — the Rockies — to their left. Cavannagh continued to curse the delay, so obsessed was he with the heavy responsibility he felt bearing down on him. Half a continent was at stake! Just as importantly, the lives of Sub-Inspector Fraser and the Baker men, of Major Walsh and thirty of his comrades at Fort Walsh, of Colonel Macleod and sixty officers and men at Fort Macleod, and ultimately of the fifty up at Fort Calgary as well.

They rode hard the remainder of the morning and

most of the afternoon. At the Milk River they lost more time looking for a suitable ford, but once they crossed and continued north toward the international boundary, the snow on the ground started giving way to a thin crust and finally disappeared altogether. Through his field glasses Cavannagh could see the dark green outline of the Cypress Hills, and closer in greater detail the long grassy plateau that they were heading for, known to the Indians as Old-Man-on-his-Back.

At sundown they passed a four-foot-high wooden post, with the words *U.S. Territory* on the south side and *British Possession* on the north.

It was high noon of the next day before Cavannagh, lying bellydown on the high, windswept grassy plateau with his field glasses pressed to his eyes, spotted movement on the broken prairie below. A dozen horsemen snaked out of one of the several long, fingerlike coulees that stretched northwesterly from the Milk River to the international boundary.

They crossed a few miles east of where Cavannagh and his three companions had crossed, and the way they traveled along the coulee bottom instead of up on the prairie surface indicated that they didn't want to be seen.

But why only twelve? Where were the others?

For half an hour Cavannagh maintained a close watch, expecting to see the remaining twenty-odd men following. But no more came. Cavannagh swept the country east and west, without sighting any more horsemen.

"Something must've gone wrong," Cavannagh muttered anxiously. "Or else they're damned sight smarter than I am."

"They're just playin' it careful-like," Dutch reassured him after he slid through the long grass at Cavannagh's beckon and peered through the glasses. "They're not ridin' overly hard."

"Can you recognize any of them?"

"I see Egg-Head—can't miss him even at this distance—an' that scarecrow ridin' aside him would be Loon-Bin. They're too far away for me to recognize the others."

"I don't think O'Shaughnessy's with them."

Schultz studied them a moment longer before handing the glasses back to Cavannagh. "I think you're right. I didn't see no red beard."

Cavannagh took the field glasses and held them to his eyes, watching the dozen horsemen moving steadily across the claylike terrain. Absorbed with his vigil, he did not pay any heed to Dutch crawling back, and hardly realized he was gone until he saw him riding down the near side of the slope toward the alkaline flats below.

"Where the hell is he going?" he called to Sergeant MacGregor, twenty or so yards back among a clump of deep green pines and autumn-bared pollars with Constable Jenkins and the horses.

"He said he was going to follow those horsemen. Seeing as he was with you there, I assumed you wanted him to."

Cavannagh shrugged and turned back to watching

181

the horsemen. I suppose he might as well, he told himself. But I hope to hell he's careful. We need every gun now.

The horsemen left the flats and headed up the grassy slopes to the trees around to the north of Old-Man-on-his-Back. They seemed to know where they were going, there was no hesitation about them. Once they got in among the thick green pines they disappeared. The last Cavannagh saw was a lone rider on a big roan galloping up from the flats after them, until he, too, was swallowed among the evergreens.

Time wore on, and Cavannagh's anxiety and impatience at Dutch's failure to return grew.

"Perhaps he might have joined them," Sergeant MacGregor suggested. "He could be warning them. After all, he was one of them nae verra long ago."

Freddie Jenkins couldn't resist throwing in his observations, especially as they could only add to Cavannagh's apprehension. "Yair . . . he's been gone a ruddy long time. 'ow far are them bah-stards goin' to go plowin' through 'eavy timber? Not too bleedin' far, by crikey." He looked suggestively at Sergeant MacGregor. "If I was the corporal, I'd 'ave me eyes peeled in case those 'orsemen come sneakin' up on us."

Sergeant MacGregor's expression was grim. "Freddie's right, Cav. They would nae go far in tha' heavy timber. They'd get lost. They must have a lair in there. If Schultz has thrown in with 'em, we're sitting in a nae verra healthy position. One of us is going tae have tae ride oot for Fort Walsh and warn the major."

"They could have caught Dutch," Cavannagh countered.

"Tha' would be just as bad. They'd know some-one's on tae them. They could make him talk. We've got tae alert the major."

Alert him to what? Cavannagh asked himself. That there's a dozen or more armed horsemen roaming through the Cypress Hills? The major could send out a strong patrol and put them to flight, but that wouldn't stop the grand scheme. It would only delay it. No! We have to smash it decisively while we have the opportunity.

Freddie's voice rasped in Cavannagh's ear.

"You've got something else to think about," and he pointed down to the undulating prairie along the border. Following the direction of Freddie's pointing arm, Cavannagh spotted movement — men and horses. Quickly he brought them closer into view with the field glasses.

Nine armed men riding across the prairie from the direction of the Milk — the Bear Paws over southeast of them. They were following the same route that Cavannagh and his party had taken, and they were crossing the border at almost exactly the same spot.

Cavannagh wondered whether they had spotted his trail! If they had . . . !

Crossing the border, the nine horsemen suddenly swung west. As they passed below the plateau, Cavannagh could make out their faces. O'Shaughnessy wasn't among them, nor Meldrum. But there was that damned half-breed with that black stovepipe hat, Buffalo Johnny. And Cavannagh thought he recognized two of the men he had arrested with Meldrum and the whisky-running outfit a month ago. They rode for two miles, until they were close to Battle Creek, then they turned north in the direction of Fort Walsh!

"That makes twenty-one. Where are the others? There should be another ten or twelve."

"Fourteen, tae be exact," Sergeant MacGregor answered. "It was thirty-five I counted that night just north of Cow Island."

Cavannagh didn't reply. This was an unexpected development; that the raiders would split up like this had never occurred to him. He had simply presumed they would keep together as one large group.

Cavannagh was sorely tempted to follow this second group, these nine horsemen, but he wanted the main lot, the one O'Shaughnessy would be with.

By sundown there had been no further movement along the border, no sign of the remainder of the raiders. As a precaution against the possibility of a surprise attack, the three Mounties moved a mile further along the plateau. Before first light the next morning they rode down off the plateau and cantered west to Battle Creek, swinging north along the same trail taken by the nine horsemen they had seen the previous afternoon, crossing the creek to the west side and pushing their horses up into thick jack pines from where they could watch the trail the bull train would take.

Fort Walsh lay thirty-five trail miles to the north.

They watched the Fort Benton trail all day, seeing nothing other than wapiti elk, deer, a few antelope, and a solitary prairie wolf slinking across the trail.

184

Again Cavannagh entertained serious doubts as to his course of action. Sergeant MacGregor entertained the same doubts, for a frown creased his brow. He clung to his opinion that one of them should ride to Fort Walsh to warn the major, but Cavannagh argued against it on the grounds that they could not afford to dilute their meager strength, and that they had nothing substantial enough to tell Major Walsh that would enable him to take effective counteraction.

"A good soldier has to decide upon the best course of action and follow it through, Mac. I needn't tell you what indecision or second thoughts can do to a battle. The same principle applies here."

The brawny Scot shook his head resignedly. "This is your case, laddie, so I'll nae throw my crown and three chevrons at ye, but I hope tae the Almighty that ye're right."

Freddie, his long lantern-jawed face bearing an expression of sheer boredom, held his tongue in the presence of these two noncommissioned officers. He was no longer enjoying Cavannagh's growing dilemma. He was becoming increasingly impatient for action, itching for the fight that something in his soldier's soul told him was coming.

They had another day and two more nights to wait. During that time they grew irritable, hungry, and at night, cold. October was nearing its end and the breath of winter was not far away. The three Mounties dared not light a campfire, for at night its glow might be seen, and by day its smoke. Without a fire they couldn't boil water for tea or coffee, nor could they cook a meal, shave, or keep warm at night.

They drank and washed in the cold waters of a nearby lake, and chewed on the last of their pemmican and beef jerky.

Then about three hours after sunrise of the third day the Baker Company bull train hove into sight along the trail from the border.

Chapter 17

Sitting their saddles at the head of a dozen heavily armed outlaws, O'Shaughnessy and Meldrum watched the Baker bull train cross the international boundary a mile ahead. Unhurriedly they followed as the train rumbled over a trail stretching northward across alkaline prairie, then with the changing terrain crawled along a shallow valley that wound between rolling, pine-dotted slopes toward the distant green bulk of the Cypress Hills.

Some two hours later O'Shaughnessy and Meldrum saw horsemen riding down the slopes toward the bull train. Putting spurs to flanks they galloped ahead. When they reached the train, Egg-Head had Mr. Fraser and the Baker men lined up beside the wagons with their hands above their heads.

Waving his long-barreled Sharps menacingly in front of the prisoners, Egg-Head greeted the red-bearded Irishman with a barbaric leer. "I'll bet there's some nice heads of hair under them hats."

Ignoring the comment. O'Shaughnessy ran his eyes

along the prisoners, stopping at Fraser. "Oi remember you. You're one of Major Walsh's officers. What are you doing here?"

Fraser sneered. "I'm representing a group of Winnipeg businessmen interested in .establishing trading—" His further words were cut off by Egg-Head who lunged forward and swung a huge fist across the young officer's face. Fraser hurtled backward, crashed against the side of a wagon, and slid unconscious to the ground. Handing his buffalo gun to Loon-Bin, Egg-Head reached for the Sioux scalping knife at his belt, leaned over and grasped Fraser's blond hair.

"That'll be enough of that, Mr. Vinsett!" the Irishman snapped.

Egg-Head looked up and glowered at the pale, red-bearded face for a moment before letting go of Fraser's hair.

O'Shaughnessy stood in his stirrups, glanced up and down the trail, then shouted to the men. "Get these wagons off the trail. We haven't time to waste."

Egg-Head thrust his scalping knife back into its sheath and took his Sharps from Loon-Bin. He kicked Fraser's limp body and snarled at two of the teamsters. "Throw him in one of them wagons."

Holding a tight rein on his prancing horse. O'Shaughnessy flung a pointed arm at the train boss. "You—get your teamsters busy movin' these wagons loike oi said. Quickly, now! No fussing around and nobody will get hurt.

With the cracking of whips and a flow of cussing,

they got the wagons rolling again. O'Shaughnessy repeatedly glanced up the trail in the direction of Fort Walsh, while the raiders rode alongside the wagons, cursing the teamsters to greater efforts.

After half a mile Egg-Head, on his great black horse, led them off the trail along a cut between two timbered slopes running at right angles to the main north-south trail. A third of a mile in, the cut curved to the left over bumpy, uneven ground for a hundred yards before leveling again. They traveled almost a mile when they came upon a broad sweep of birch and willow-clumped flat walled in by pined hills. It would have looked tantalizingly beautiful in the full green of spring and summer, and in the gold of September, but now in mid-Octobter it was a lifeless brown. Beside one of the willow clumps stood a line of picketed mules and four U.S. Army wagons, three with gray canvas covers, the fourth covered by orange canvas so bright that it offended the eye. Six armed men, typical Missouri desperadoes, lounged about, most of them smoking, obviously waiting for Egg-Head and the new arrivals.

"Swing 'em around, wagon master," O'Shaughnessy sang out, circling with his arm.

The train boss yelled to the teamsters and they drove the oxen and wagons around in a wide semicircle.

O'Shaughnessy stood in his stirrups and shouted. "Now everyone pitch in and unload the wagons. And hurry it oop. We haven't any toime to lose."

With Egg-Head's intimidating bulk looming over

them, his long buffalo gun ready to swing out and crack the tardy, outlaws and teamsters climbed up into the wagons and quickly tossed the ammunition boxes in an untidy heap into the center of the semicircle.

It took considerably less time to unload the wagons than it had taken to load them at Cow Island, and when they were finished Egg-Head herded together the teamsters and the now-conscious Fraser, blood caked around his mouth. The outlaws tied their hands behind their backs, and at O'Shaughnessy's order, unsaddled their horses, then hobbled them on the flat to graze. Four men went over behind the army wagons, reappearing a moment later carrying a Hotchkiss breech-loader.

"Put that in the first wagon," O'Shaughnessy directed, pointing to the lead Baker wagon.

The four outlaws obeyed, while the remainder, trailing rifles and slinging ammunition bandoliers over their shoulders, sauntered toward the empty Baker wagons.

"Distribute yourselves evenly among the wagons," shouted O'Shaughnessy. "Don't forget the Hotchkiss shells." Then to Egg-Head he said, "Leave three men to watch the prisoners."

Egg-Head replied, "It's the horses that have to be watched. The prisoners we kill."

O'Shaughnessy shook his head. "Not yet. Oi don't want the sound of shots rolling around the Cypress Hills until three days have passed. Oi want nothing to forewarn the redcoats."

Egg-Head argued. "You said Fort Walsh is thirty-five miles away. They won't hear shots that far off."

"A patrol might be within hearing distance, or some Indians. We can't afford to take the chance."

Egg-Head drew his scalping knife and leered. "Egg-Head fix 'em. Noise, there won't be none—except their screamin'." And he burst into a convulsing belly laugh.

O'Shaughnessy, unamused, shook his head firmly. "No. They'll be killed decently, loike Christians. A bullet in the head for each of them. Now be good enough to attend to it. And remember, tell whoever you leave behind—no shots for three days."

For the second time that day Egg-Head thrust his scalping knife back into its sheath, this time more grudgingly. Glancing around the wagons, he bellowed. "Cousins. Come!" and pointed a thick finger at the ground in front of him.

Obediently, Cousins jumped down from the tailgate of one of the canvas-covered Baker wagons and trotted forward. The month-old scar on his forehead just below his hairline showed quite visibly under his pushed-back hat.

"You watch the prisoners. Three days time, you kill. Savvy?"

Cousins nodded. Egg-Head turned to the gray scarecrow hovering, as always, right behind him. "Loon-Bin, you stay with him. He does what I say, you make sure."

Loon-Bin cackled. "Sure thing, Egg-Head. Whatever you say, Egg-Head."

Egg-Head called to a third man. "You watch the horses 'til we get back."

"How long'll that be, Egg-Head?" the man asked.

"Four days — when we come back for the beauty in there," said Egg-Head, pointing at the orange-covered wagon.

The outlaws had now settled themselves into the Baker wagons, with one or two sitting at the front of each. O'Shaughnessy and Meldrum paced along counting them. Thirty-two — every one armed with a Winchester repeating rifle, at least one pistol and sometimes two, and lots of ammunition.

O'Shaughnessy frowned. "Oi wish we had a dozen more."

Meldrum belched. "Countin' me, yew an' Egg-Head, we got thirty-five an' the Hotchkiss. Afore we git to Fort Walsh, we'll pick up Buffalo Johnny, Yates, an' Daniels. That'll make thirty-eight. These boys are the best guns on the Missouri plains. There's only thirty redcoats at Fort Walsh. We'll take 'em at sundown, right when they're all packed together in a nice tidy parade formation fer their retreat ceremony. And I'm lookin forward to thet. I've got a score to settle with them British-lovin' bastards fer puttin' me in thet damn jail of theirs."

Meldrum's words restored the Irishman's confidence and his red-bearded face opened in a grin. "Yes. In fact, when they see the wagons they'll breathe sighs of relief because they'll think its the delivery of their precious bullets."

O'Shaughnessy paused for a moment, adding, "It'll

192

be bullets all roight — but those damned redcoats will be gettin' them in a manner they'll not be wantin'."

He turned and shouted to Egg-Head, who waved his Sharps in reply, ambled over to the nearest wagon, pushed one of the men sitting on the seat backward into the wagon box, and hauled his huge body up onto the first wagon. Meldrum cracked the whip over the oxen's backs and the wagons lurched forward toward the Fort Walsh trail.

Chapter 18

From high up on the pine-covered slope of the south hill, Cavannagh and MacGregor looked down on the snakelike wagon train rumbling along the cut below to the Fort Walsh trail. They could see O'Shaughnessy, easily recognizable by his red beard, seated on the lead wagon, and further back the monstrous bulk of Egg-Head.

They had watched the bull train from the moment it crossed the border into the North West Territories, and had seen the outlaws jump it and drive it off into the hills. They had watched the armed outlaws throw the ammunition cases out of the wagons, and replace them with the Hotchkiss. Now, with the wagons rattling back along the cut between the two hills, MacGregor voiced the thought puzzling them both.

"Why the bluidy hell are they riding in those damned slow wagons when they have all that good horseflesh back there?"

The answer hit Cavannagh like a flash!

"Didn't you tell me that when O'Shaughnessy was at Fort Walsh he drew sketches of the interior of the fort?"

"Aye."

Cavannagh's voice shook with excitement. "Then that's it! O'Shaughnessy is going to get his outlaws inside Fort Walsh under the cover of those ammunitions wagons. They'll take the troop completely by surprise. They'll shoot them down in cold blood!"

"That's bluidy murder!"

Thank God April isn't there, Cavannagh thought. To MacGregor he said, "At least now we know their plan."

"Noo we can warn the major."

"First we have to get Fraser and the Baker men loose."

Below them the bull train rumbled on around the bend. They waited until it reached the main trail and turned north toward Fort Walsh. Then they rode back through the pines to a point above the willow and birch flat, where Freddie Jenkins watched the camp. Leaving their horses in his care, they crept down the slope, keeping under cover until they nearly reached the flat. They were trying to decide how to cross the remaining distance of a hundred yards without running the risk of gunfire when they spotted movement among the bare trees behind the orange-covered wagon.

When Cavannagh grabbed MacGregor's wrist and wordlessly pointed, they both crouched down into some underbrush and watched.

A man in a leather jacket crawled out of the trees and darted unnoticed by the three outlaws across the clearing to the orange-covered wagon. The next instant he stepped around from behind the wagon and pointed his Winchester at them.

Dutch Schultz!

At a sharp command from Schultz the outlaws stretched their arms above their heads and turned around. Then he looked over to where Cavannagh and MacGregor crouched in the underbrush.

"Come on out, Cavannagh," he yelled. "I got 'em."

Cavannagh and Sergeant MacGregor exchanged glances, rose to their full height, and stepped out of the brush, walking across the flat to where the grinning Schultz awaited them.

Cavannagh was about to ask Schultz how he knew they were up there, but Dutch saved him the trouble.

"I told you how I'm gettin' to know the way you do things. Anyways, I saw you and that big Scotchman up on the opposite hill watchin' the bull train, an' I knew you'd come back here to let your officer loose, just like I knew you'd come down that slope and run out of cover, riskin' one of these critters goin' for a gun. So I figgered I'd better do the job for you. Otherwise, all them raiders over on the north trail'd be swarmin' back here right now."

Cavannagh nodded. "Thanks, Dutch. You're handy to have around. I have some questions to ask you, but right now there isn't time."

Sergeant MacGregor had hurried over to Sub-Inspector Fraser and cut the ropes binding him. "Are ye all right, sirr?"

Fraser rubbed his wrists and tenderly touched his swollen face. "Yes, I think so, Sergeant."

"We must warn Major Walsh that these outlaws are on their way tae attack the fort, sirr," MacGregor said.

Cavannagh joined them. "O'Shaughnessy plans to wipe out Fort Macleod as well, but we don't know how he intends doing it."

"Then we had better find out," Fraser said. "And quickly!"

The three outlaws, their eyes darting from one speaker to the other, listened. Cavannagh turned to face them.

"You three must know. How does O'Shaughnessy plan to attack Fort Macleod?"

None of the three answered. Schultz, standing behind them with the pointed Winchester, suddenly cracked Loon-Bin a stinging blow on the side of the head with the rifle barrel.

"Speak up, Loon-Bin, you scarecrow, son of a bitch. You must know. You're Egg-Head's shadow."

"You go plumb t' hell, Schultz!" Loon-Bin spat. "You're a marked man. Egg-Head will git you."

Schultz laughed, then poked his rifle in Cousins's back. "Open up your big mouth, Cousins. You always was a blabbermouth. Tell the man what he wants to know."

The scarecrow cackled. "Don't tell 'em nothin', Cousins. Egg-Head'll git us outta this."

Schultz cracked Loon-Bin across the side of the head again. "Shut up, you miserable old Johnny Reb throwback."

"O'Shaughnessy will never get away with this," Cavannagh told the three prisoners. "He and those outlaws will never reach Fort Walsh except in chains. You men tell me exactly what his plans are and I'll do everything in my power to see that you get lighter sentences for cooperating. Otherwise, you face the hangman's rope."

Dutch Schultz said to Cavannagh, "If you go over to that wagon with the orange tarp and have a peek inside, mebbe you'll get your answer in there."

Cavannagh strode over to the orange covered wagon. Untying the lashings, he jerked aside the tarp flaps and looked inside. A long, low whistle escaped his lips. Sub-Inspector Fraser joined him and looked over his shoulder, his eyebrows rising at the sight of a twelve-pounder field gun, complete with cases of shells and barrels of gunpowder.

Leaving Sergeant MacGregor to watch the prisoners, Dutch Schultz ambled over to the wagon.

"Notice anythin' strange about this wagon? It comes apart and that section up front becomes a gun carriage. This here's why I didn't come back to Old-Man-on-his-Back. I follered that first bunch into the hills. They struck a trail and cut north of the plateau until they came here. They knowed where they was headin', and this thing was waitin' for 'em, together with these other wagons and six men. They been doin' some dry drills with it. I guess they would've practiced, only they didn't want the noise to carry up to Fort Walsh." He scratched the back of his neck. "Thing I don't understand, though, is why they didn't take it with 'em."

Cavannagh said, "What they're doing is more effective. They must have intended using this gun at first, then came up with a better—" He stopped in midsentence. *"No!* That's how they intend taking Fort Macleod. They'll shell it."

198

"Fort Macleod has field guns," Sub-Inspector Fraser said. "They could return the fire.

A cackling sounded from among the three prisoners. Old Loon-Bin was nearly convulsed with barely suppressed laughter.

"You're purty smart, young fella. Purty danged smart you are. But you ain't got it figgered yet. No sirree. Hey-hey-heh."

"We're wasting time, sirr," Sergeant MacGregor called from where he was still watching the three prisoners. "We must get word tae the major."

Cavannagh stood thinking furiously, fidgeting with the dark beard stubble on his chin.

"Where is Constable Jenkins, Sergeant?" Sub-Inspector Fraser asked.

"Up on the slope, sirr. With our horses."

"Get him down here."

"Aye, sirr." Sergeant MacGregor cast a warning glance at the prisoners, then looked up the slope, cupped his hands over his mouth, and shouted. A few minutes later Freddie rode down out of the trees with the horses.

From the orange-topped wagon, Cavannagh suddenly shouted out triumphantly. *"A relief column!* O'Shaughnessy intends faking a message to Fort Macleod that Fort Walsh is under attack. With only sixty men, Colonel Macleod will have to send almost his entire command. O'Shaughnessy will wait for them with the Hotchkiss and this twelve-pounder. He'll blow them to pieces!"

"Hey-hey-heh!" Loon-Bin cackled. "Yes, sirree . . . that young fella sure is danged smart."

Sergeant MacGregor and Dutch Schultz tied the prisoners, then Sub-Inspector Fraser called the men around him.

"It's up to us to stop these outlaws. One of us will ride to Fort Walsh and alert the major. The remainder will follow the wagons and hold themselves in readiness to assist B Troop when it arrives. More than likely there'll be a fight. I don't imagine O'Shaughnessy will surrender." The sub-inspector looked at Dutch Schultz. "I presume we can count you in with us, Mr. Schultz?"

Schultz grinned. "I wouldn't be missin' it, Inspector."

"Good." Fraser glanced over at the Baker men who had been released and were standing in a knot. "What about your men, wagon master? We have two spare rifles. Two volunteers would be much appreciated."

The train boss stepped forward. "I'll go." He looked around at his men. "How about you fellers? Deke?"

The one addressed as Deke dug his toe into the ground. "I dunno," he said, shaking his head slowly. "I gotta walk these trails with the bulls. We could run inter these fellas agin. If'n it gits around that we took part in a'huntin' 'em down up here in Canady, we could be marked men."

One of the other teamsters stepped forward. "Count me in."

"Thank you, gentlemen," said Sub-Inspector Fraser. "Take a Winchester each and saddle two of the outlaws' horses."

Leaving the remaining teamsters to watch the three

200

outlaw prisoners, Sub-Inspector Fraser led his small force along the cut between the two hills back to the Fort Walsh trail. When they reached it, they reined to and the officer turned to Cavannagh.

"Those outlaws must be four or five miles up the trail by now. I understand that you know these hills as well as any man in B Troop. Corporal. How readily can one of us bypass the trail where those wagons would be, and carry on to Fort Walsh?"

Cavannagh glanced up the trail to the hills rising on either side. Pointing, he replied, "Cut up over that second slope. There's a depression about half a mile on the far side. Follow it until it meets Battle Creek flowing in from the west, then stay beside the creek until it turns to come down from the north. From there the trail takes you directly to Fort Walsh."

"Thank you, Corporal." Sub-Inspector Fraser twisted in his saddle to face the others. "I require a volunteer to ride north with a message for Major Walsh."

Cavannagh said, "In my opinion, sir, it would be best if you go. You're an officer. You could provide the major with the best report. And if he and Sub-Inspector Allen should both be absent from the post, you have the rank to turn out the troop."

The blond sub-inspector thought about this for a moment. "Very well. I'll go. I'll follow the route you indicated, Corporal. We should meet again by tomorrow morning."

"Take my horse, sir," Cavannagh said, dismounting. "If you lose your way, just let him have his head. He'll find the way."

Cavannagh handed his reins to the officer. Sub-Inspector Fraser jumped down from the horse he was on and hauled himself up into Cavannagh's saddle.

"Good luck, sir."

"Good luck to you, men," replied Mr. Fraser, and the next instant the big bay broke into a canter and headed north.

Chapter 19

Too impatient to merely sit on the jolting, hard, uncomfortable wagon seat, Michael O'Shaughnessy walked alongside the lead wagon. Not that walking would get him and his raiders to Fort Walsh any faster, but the exercise helped to curb his impatience.

Egg-Head Vinsett, afflicted with the same ailment, lumbered along beside him.

"Are we goin' to push all night?"

"No!" O'Shaughnessy snapped back.

"Why not? We gotta cover a lotta distance yet, and we ain't got much time."

"Shut oop and do what you're told!"

Egg-Head jerked his head sideways to glare at O'Shaughnessy. No one else dared say anything like that to him. If they did he'd have their scalp. But this damned Irishman was the Colonel's man, so Egg-Head slung his Sharps over his shoulder and

sulked along a few feet behind O'Shaughnessy in
brooding silence.

Cavannagh rode slowly among the pines high up
on the side of a hill and looked down on the bull
train rumbling along the trail below. Sergeant Mac-
Gregor followed a horse-length behind, while Dutch
Schultz, Freddie Jenkins, and the two Baker men
kept out of sight further back.

"How fast do ye reckon they're traveling?"

"Two miles an hour, if that. Less than the Baker
bullwhackers would do."

"Even so, they're nae doin' too bad. Those oxen
dinna look tae me the easiest beasts in the world tae
handle."

"At that rate it'll take them about fifteen hours to
reach Fort Walsh. There's another hour of daylight
left. If they move all night, they'll be at the fort
sometime before noon tomorrow."

"Aye, but Mr. Fraser should gain the fort before
midnight. The troop can be doon the trail and
positioned tae stop that murderous riffraff by
dawn."

The sky was turning crimson behind the hills to
the west as Sub-Inspector Fraser galloped Cavannagh's big bay gelding northward along the Fort
Walsh trail. He was pleased with the progress he had

204

made, better than he had expected. He was familiar with this stretch of the trail and knew the fort was less than an hour away. Once there, he would have time for a quick meal before exchanging the bay for a fresh mount and returning southward with B Troop to attack the outlaws at dawn.

Yes, he was well pleased with himself. He had made good progress indeed.

Suddenly, out of the corner of his eye he caught a snakelike blur of movement over his head and the next instant he was abruptly jerked clean out of the saddle as a lasso tightened around his shoulders. He landed on his rump with a spine-jarring thud that knocked the wind out of him. Before he could struggle to his feet, he found himself dragged along the ground and heard the drumming of horse hoofs from behind.

The last thing he saw before he was clubbed into unconsciousness was a half-breed wearing a tall black stovepipe hat riding furiously along the trail to overtake Cavannagh's running bay.

The sun had been down for two hours when Meldrum, cracking his whip uselessly over the lead team for the umpteenth time, spat in disgust.

"These damn bulls is balkin' all the time now, Mr. O'Shaughnessy. We ain't goin' to get much more out of them tonight."

O'Shaughnessy grunted. "All roight. Pull them

off to the soide of the trail. We'll go on first thing in the morning."

"This is far enough fer the day," Meldrum shouted down the line of wagons. "Pull 'em over and make camp." He needed the rest. So did the others.

But not Egg-Head. He stormed up out of the darkness.

"What the hell are we stoppin' for?"

"The animals," O'Shaughnessy answered.

"T' hell with the animals!"

Feeling more conciliatory than he had earlier, O'Shaughnessy replied, "They're balking. There's no point in driving them all noight and exhausting them by morning. We need them just as mooch tomorrow as today. We've coom far enough, anyway. We'll have enough toime tomorrow to get to Fort Walsh just before sundown. Then we'll stroike."

Egg-Head grinned. Even in the darkness, O'Shaughnessy could see the flash of his teeth, and wondered if the monstrous pervert was thinking of all the scalps he could take.

O'Shaughnessy added, "Then we can take care of the redcoats at Fort Macleod. With the twelve-pounder and the Hotchkiss, we'll be able to handle them noicely out on the open prairie."

Meldrum asked, "What about the fifty men further north up on the Bow?"

"They'll be so oisolated they won't matter. Maybe the Indians will woipe them out once they know the others are dead. The moighty magic of the British

206

red tunic will be smashed. The Indians will see it for what it is—a big bluff."

Through his field glasses Cavannagh watched the outlaws' campfires alongside the trail below. He could see O'Shaughnessy and the bald-headed giant in buckskin sitting and eating around one of the fires.

Not much noise drifted up the slope, nor was there much movement from the outlaws once they finished eating. Most of them stretched into their blankets beside the wagons. Two or three sat around smoking before turning in. Four or five stood guard, spread along the length of the motionless train, rifles cradled in their arms or held by their sides.

Cavannagh lowered the glasses. "It must be about nine o'clock."

MacGregor fumbled in his coat pocket and produced a gold-plated pocket watch, a carefully protected family possession. He flipped open the case front and peered at the glass dial.

"I canna read it in the dark, and I dinna think I should strike a match."

Cavannagh shook his head in the blackness. "It doesn't matter. I was just thinking that in another couple of hours Fraser should reach Fort Walsh. The major and B Troop should be here by sunrise. I think I had better ride north a little and guide them in. They'll have to take up positions. We don't want them stumbling blindly onto this bunch."

"Guid plan. I'll go with ye. Freddie, Schultz, and two Baker men can stay up here and watch. Then when the troop moves in frae the north, they can cover the rear and cut off any attempt at escape tae the south."

Chapter 20

Outlaws were attacking Fort Walsh, shelling it with the field gun and the Hotchkiss. The buildings were ablaze, redcoats were falling, and April Bannister, her golden hair vivid against the backdrop of flames, stood calling Cavannagh's name.

Then Cavannagh awakened, fighting down a sense of despair, until he realized it had only been a dream, that April was safe from immediate harm five hundred miles away at Fort Edmonton.

Cold and cramped, he looked up at the morning sky, streaked with the gray of first light. He threw off his blankets and climbed stiffly to his feet. Sergeant MacGregor leaned against a jack pine, silently watching the trail to the north. Their horses stood saddled nearby.

"What's happening?" Cavannagh asked huskily.

"Nothing," MacGregor replied dourly.

Alarm sprang into Cavannagh's voice. "Where the hell is B Troop?"

MacGregor hook his head. "I dinna know. There's nae any sign of them."

"They should be here by now. You should have woken me."

"It would nae hae served any purpose. Besides, ye needed the sleep."

Cavannagh was silent for a moment. Then he heard rumbling and the crack of whips coming along the trail from the south. The bull train—it was on the move again.

"Something's gone wrong! B Troop should have been here long ago."

"They must've got off tae a late start."

"No, Mac. You know it as well as I do. Major Walsh would be here now if Fraser had reached the fort."

"*If* he'd reached—?"

Cavannagh didn't let him finish. "He was intercepted. I should have realized it, that O'Shaughnessy has men watching the fort. Prefontaine and I found tracks."

The big Scot exploded. "Well, then, we'd better get somebody else on the way there immediately."

Cavannagh shook his head impatiently. "The same thing would happen again. We don't know how many men are watching the fort or where they are. We have to try something else."

"Such as?"

"We have to stop O'Shaughnessy ourselves."

"Hoo? We dinna hae neither the men nor the firepower."

Cavannagh rubbed his beard-length whiskers. "Damn it all! If there had only been some rifles with that ammunition shipment, or better still some spare Winchesters back at that camp, we could have armed those remaining Baker men and tried an ambush."

"Back at that camp," MacGregor repeated. Then

his eyes lit up. *"The field gun!"*

Cavannagh shook his head. "We're cavalrymen, not gunners."

A wide grin covered Sergeant MacGregor's face. "But Mrs. Jenkins's little boy, Freddie, was. He came into the Mounted Police frae the School of Gunnery at Kingston."

Cavannagh gave the handsome Scot a hard look. "Can he handle American army ordnance?"

"Freddie was an Imperial regular, Cavannagh—a gunner in the British Army. Aye, he can handle it."

"It's a long ride back to that camp."

"Aye, but nae too far. Freddie and I will go get the gun. You, Schultz, and the two Baker men watch those bastards below."

MacGregor sprang up into his saddle with the agility of a man fifteen years younger, wheeled his horse around, and with a quick jab of spurs, showed Cavannagh the animal's hoofs.

Troop Sergeant-Major Francis, resplendent in scarlet tunic and white helmet, emerged from Major Walsh's quarters beside the east gates and marched smartly around the parade ground toward the log stables over against the west palisade. The jingle of spurs and the clank of steel-scabbarded sword accompanied him.

Arriving at the stables, his soldierly presence filled the doorway. The constable in charge of the morning fatigue party clicked the heels of his urine-stained stable boots together, stiffened his arms by his sides, and arched his back.

211

"Good morning, sir."

The sergeant-major nodded. "Morning, Akroyd."

The fatigue party, aware of the august presence, worked that much harder—mucking out stalls, sweeping straw down the center aisles, currycombing horses. Sergeants-major breathed fire, especially when they detected lazy men.

"Any sick or lame horses, Akroyd?"

"No, sir. None."

"Good. Has the day's issue of forage been inspected for quality?"

"Yes, sir."

"Any mounts requiring shoeing?"

"Two, sir."

"Very well. See that the acting farrier-major is so informed. And at the conclusion of stable parade, turn over your troop duties to the next senior man. Immediately after breakfast get into full service order and tell off Scout Prefontaine for duty. You and he will patrol south along the Benton trail until you meet a Baker bull train carrying the force's ammunition supplies. Mr. Fraser will be with it. You are to convey to him Major Walsh's compliments and inform him that he may return to the fort forthwith. You will take a spare saddle horse, which you will turn over to him. Take field rations for three days. You shouldn't be gone any longer than that. Got it?"

"Yes, sir."

"Good. Carry on."

Sergeant-Major Francis then executed a perfect drill-manual about-turn and marched out of the stables and back around the barrack square toward the east palisade.

* * *

The golden sun hovered straight above at high noon as Cavannagh, up among the jack pines, glared down impotently upon the relentlessly moving bull train with its deadly cargo of heavily armed desperadoes, rumbling ominously closer and closer to an unsuspecting Fort Walsh.

Taut with impatience, Cavannagh's knuckles whitened as they gripped his Winchester.

"Come on, Jenkins—*damn you*! Get here with that cursed gun!"

Chapter 21

The sudden screeching whistle of a twelve-pound shell rocketing through the air startled Cavannagh's tension-tightened nerves. So did the explosion that followed. A red flash and a billowy cloud of black and yellow smoke erupted a few feet behind the last wagon, frightening the lumbering oxen into bolting with their tandem of wagons and smashing them into the tandem ahead. Startled yells and curses rose into the air as outlaws spilled from the canvas-covered vehicles.

Cavannagh hurled himself behind a thick pine, threw his Winchester up to his shoulder, and opened fire. A couple of trees away stood the Baker train boss, doing the same. Across the valley on the opposite slope, Dutch Schultz and the bullwhacker were also firing down on the wagons.

Amid the confusion, outlaws tumbled out of the other wagons, their eyes peering up the slopes searching for targets on which to sight their rifles. The men below fell to the ground as Cavannagh triggered his Winchester, but by the time he levered his last round into the breech, the outlaws had spotted him and were firing back, bullets peeling bark off the jack pine.

Squeezing off his last round, Cavannagh pulled back behind the pine as several bullets bit into it. One singed his thigh; he jammed himself hard against the tree.

"Come on, Jenkins!" Cavannagh muttered, sliding fresh cartridges into the loading slot. "Get that field gun firing again!"

A bullet found the Baker train boss, and cursing and clutching his shoulder, he slid down behind his tree.

"How badly are you hit?" Cavannagh called out to him.

"It hurts some," the train boss called back. "I don't reckon I can hold a gun into my shoulder."

"Can you load?"

"Reckon so," the train boss shouted back, his voice barely audible above the noise of crashing rifles.

"Then load your Winchester and toss it to me."

A second twelve-pound shell screeched through the air to land right into the lead wagon, blowing it to pieces. With it went the Hotchkiss. Risking a bullet in the head, Cavannagh peered around the tree in time to see bodies flying in the air. One was O'Shaughnessy's.

Pandemonium broke out among the outlaws at this unexpected and devastating attack. Instead of handing out deathly surprise, they were receiving it. But Egg-Head, raging and bellowing like a huge bull, drove them scrambling up the slopes to seek out their attackers.

Cavannagh caught the train boss's thrown Winchester and darted to another tree to fire down on the outlaws clambering up the slope. He emptied one

Winchester, all but one of his bullets finding targets, and slowed them down, while Dutch Schultz, firing from the opposite slope, killed two more. Cavannagh returned the favor by opening up on three of the outlaws who were trying to make their way up to Schultz's position. Despite Egg-Head's urging, the others slunk back to cover under the wagons, only to run wildly as the field gun's third shell hit one of the middle wagons and blew it to smithereens!

The oxen panicked, bolting with the wagons, trampling men underfoot. There were screams, curses, and the cracking of rifles, as more outlaws fell. A bullet from Egg-Head's long-barreled Sharps ended the life of the Baker bullwhacker up on the slope with Schultz. Then the Sharps moved over to Schultz's tree. Its distinctive boom reverberated up the slope, and a .45 bullet tore into the bark one inch from Schultz's chest.

Cavannagh used all the bullets in the train boss's Winchester and pulled back to feed fresh cartridges into both rifles. Bullets thudded into the tree behind him, and another singed him, this time in the buttock. Cavannagh twisted around to fire at whoever had loosed that shot, realizing from the angle of fire that one of the outlaws was flanking him. He spotted the crouching man—Droopy Moustache Meldrum! But before he could bring up his Winchester to aim, a shot cracked from the opposite slope and Meldrum staggered upright for an instant and then toppled backward down the pine-dotted slope. Looking across to the other slope, Cavannagh saw Schultz wave at him with his rifle.

Another shell from the twelve-pounder screeched

through the air and burst into the ground between two wagons, blowing them apart. From the slope Cavannagh could see MacGregor and Jenkins with the smoking field gun. They had moved it closer to get better aim, but no more cannon shells were necessary. The second and third had done enough damage, together with the rampaging oxen and Cavannagh's and Schultz's deadly marksmanship. Now the few remaining outlaws, dazed, were dropping their rifles and raising their hands in surrender. There were no more than five or six; the rest either dead, wounded, or injured.

Except for one man!

Egg-Head knelt on one knee beside a broken wagon, brought his Sharps up to his shoulder, and took deliberate aim on Dutch Schultz's tree. He squeezed the trigger, and the long-barreled buffalo gun bucked heavily, belching flame and smoke. Schultz dropped his Winchester and grabbed at his chest. Bright red blood spilled over his hands as he sank slowly to the ground. Egg-Head, the broad-bladed Sioux scalping knife in his hand, raced up the slope toward Schultz like a charging grizzly.

He was halfway up the slope when Cavannagh caught him with a .44-40 from his Winchester, but the buckskin-clothed giant hardly faltered. Urgently, Cavannagh levered the Winchester and fired again. As the second bullet rammed into him Egg-Head staggered, but uttering a piercing yell that seemed to give him renewed energy, he continued on his scalp-crazed charge uphill.

Cavannagh's third bullet, which drilled a hole right in the back of the bald egg-shaped head, finally toppled the gargantuan outlaw who landed dead, only a foot away from Schultz. His scalping knife fell out of his hand and rolled a dozen yards down the slope.

Cavannagh and Sergeant MacGregor reached the shattered wagons at the same time.

"Dutch has been shot, Mac. Watch the prisoners, will you?"

The big Scot scowled at the half-dozen dazed prisoners as Cavannagh dashed off up the hill toward Schultz.

Schultz met Cavannagh with a weak, blood-smeared grin. "Thanks, Lieutenant. I didn't wanna die . . ." A fit of coughing convulsed him as he spewed forth frothy blood. Cavannagh yanked his yellow cavalry bandanna from around his neck and wiped the blood and mucus from Schultz's mouth.

Schultz grinned again. His words came with a rasping effort. "Didn't wanna . . . die without . . . my scalp. I'm glad . . . you killed that queer-lookin' son of a bitch. I'm glad you did it for me. It's sorta . . . sorta like I did it myself. That . . . that's a score settled. I got Meldrum . . . you saw that, didn't you, Lieutenant?"

Cavannagh nodded. "I saw it, Dutch."

Schultz coughed again. Cavannagh tried to turn him around to make him comfortable, but Schultz managed to shake his head.

"Don't bother . . . I ain't got much time left. One thing more . . . git that half-Crow son of a bitch . . . Buffalo Johnny. He's rotten bad. Tried to double-cross me. He's gotta be around here somewheres."

"I'll get him, Dutch. I want him anyway."

"Yeah . . . I know. You'll get him . . . I know you will."

Dutch closed his eyes. His breathing seemed to come easier now. "That Colonel fella . . . you don't have to worry about him none. I killed him before . . . we left the riverboat."

He coughed, more feebly, and managing another grin he said, "You did it, Cavannagh . . . you stopped 'em and saved the country you're servin'. That Mounted Police outfit got themselves a good man when they took you on."

Schultz raised his hand and threw off a feeble salute.

Tears in his eyes, Cavannagh saluted him back. "So long, *Captain*."

Chapter 22

Constable Akroyd and Scout Prefontaine were a
hour out of Fort Walsh when they heard the firs
crashing explosion of the field gun, followed by th
rattle of rifle fire.

"What the devil!" Akroyd exclaimed, tuggin
sharply on his horse's reins.

"*Sacre Dieu*!" uttered the *Metis* scout.

More rifle shots sounded down the trail, the an
other crashing explosion.

The *Metis*'s black eyes widened in shock. "D
ammunition, she ees blowing up!"

Constable Akroyd shook his head. "No! That's
cannon. Come on." He put spurs to his horse.

"Mebbe we better get 'elp from d' fort?" Jule
Prefontaine shouted after him.

Akroyd shouted back over his shoulder. "They'
hear it. Come on."

Jules thumped the barrellike sides of his prairi
cayuse and the wiry little animal flew after the large
troop horse and its red-coated rider.

But suddenly the redcoat pitched from his saddle
Jules heard the report of a rifle and swerved hi

cayuse to miss hurtling into the rolling Akroyd.

Another shot echoed from the pine-covered slopes and Jules realized someone was shooting at him. Swining his cayuse up the opposite slope, he zig-zagged wildly to make a harder target.

Akroyd stopped rolling. Dazedly pulling himself to a sitting position, he shook his head to clear his senses, reaching across his body, and drew his heavy service revolver. A bullet furrowed into the ground beside him. Ignoring it, he pointed his revolver up the slope to where the shots came from and in as many seconds emptied all six chambers.

Jules reached the protection of trees and skidded his cayuse to a dirt-showering halt. Jerking his Snider from its saddle bucket, he cocked and aimed at the other slope.

He glimped movement and fired, missed, reloaded, and fired again. Shots were returned, one nicking the cayuse, which jumped but wasn't hurt. Jules knew from the rapidity of the return fire that he was up against repeating rifles in the hands of two or three men.

He peered down to the trail and saw Akroyd reloading his revolver. The constable was completely exposed and very conspicuous in his bright red coat. He was still sitting, making no attempt to move, so Jules figured he must have hurt his leg when he came off his horse. He watched Akroyd open fire up at the trees on the opposite slope again, but the range was too great for his revolver. However, the riflemen weren't firing back.

The black-bearded *Metis* moved slightly. Bullets peppered his tree. Now he knew why the riflemen weren't bothering with Akroyd. They were too busy trying to kill him. He wished desperately that he had a Winchester repeater instead of a single-shot Snider.

Suddenly, across on the opposite slope, a horse broke out of the trees. One of the riflemen made a move to grab its reins. Jules recognized Cavannagh's big bay gelding. He whipped his carbine up to his shoulder and fired, and the rifleman spun around and fell. Quickly Jules reloaded.

There was more firing and another explosion from south along the trail, but no more shots came from the opposite slope. Jules cautiously inched his head around the tree. Nothing happened, so he darted to another tree, then another. No shots followed him. He was wondering why when two horsemen galloped out of the pines on the far slope and tore recklessly southward in a diagonal line down to the trail below. In a blur of movement, Jules aimed and fired. One of the saddles emptied. The other horsemen kept on going.

"*Mon Dieu!*" Jules muttered. He recognized the escaping horseman by his description. A half-breed in a tall black stovepipe hat.

Cavannagh had just finished burying Dutch Schultz in the shadow of a lonesome pine towering above a jutting point on the hill where he had fought his last fight, and was descending to the valley below

222

when he heard wild shouting and pounding hoofs. Looking down he saw two horsemen riding fast along the trail from the direction of Fort Walsh. Behind them tailed a riderless horse. He identified the shouting before the riders were close enough for him to recognize Jules Prefontaine and Sub-Inspector Fraser towing his bay.

He ran the rest of the way to the trail below, where Sergeant MacGregor and a triumphantly grinning Freddie Jenkins stood guard over the handful of prisoners and the wounded and injured sitting or lying among the shambles and litter of dead men, splintered wagons, and broken wheels. Sub-Inspector Fraser and Jules reined to in front of them.

" 'ey, Cavannagh, *mon ami*," the scout whooped delightedly at seeing his friend, bearded and haggard but alive and well. "Ha-ha! They no keel, you, huh!"

Sub-Inspector Fraser looked around, quickly taking in the scene of destruction.

"Damned good work, men. Damned good, indeed."

Jules leaned forward in his saddle and spoke excitedly to Cavannagh. "*Mon ami*, dat 'alf-breed in d' black 'at, I see 'eem jus' a little while back." He pointed up at the pines lining the slopes. " 'e ees up dere, tryin' to get around you. He ees 'eadin' for d' Montana border. You wan' to get 'eem, *non*?"

Cavannagh's steel-blue eyes hardened. "You're damned right I want him, Jules."

Hefting his Winchester, Cavannagh reached for the bay's reins and sprang up into the saddle. Then he turned to the officer. "With your permission, sir?"

Sub-Inspector Fraser's aristocratic mouth curved into a smile. "You have it, Corporal."

Making a clicking noise with his mouth, Cavannagh spoke to his horse. "Come on, boy," and the animal hammered up the grassed slope toward the pines. Without bothering to ask for permission, Jules urged his wiry cayuse up the slope right behind him.

They reached the trees and slowed their horses to a walk while Jules studied the ground. But it was Cavannagh who spotted tracks first. The scout beamed at his friend, admiration in his bright black eyes.

" 'ey, you gettin' pretty damn good, *mon ami*. Pretty soon you no need scout."

"Beginner's luck, Jules. Come on, let's get after him."

The tracks led on through the trees, then over the hill and down the other side. Cavannagh could follow them as long as they stayed on the needle-covered ground, but once they left the pines and crossed open grass patches he had to rely on Jules.

Buffalo Johnny's trail led south, then veered southwest. Cavannagh thought he was heading out of the Cypress Hills, making for rolling prairie to the west. That would give him more direct access to Fort Benton—if that was where he was going—cutting off as much as a day's travel. But then the tracks turned south again, so Cavannagh realized the half-breed was going to stay within the cover of the treed hills.

The afternoon wore on. A buildup of heavy black

224

clouds gathered in the west. It portended snow. That could be either good or bad, depending upon where it fell, and whether or not in the form of a blizzard. It could help them track Buffalo Johnny, or it could help him escape altogether. Approaching nightfall could also aid his escape.

They sighted Buffalo Johnny once, crossing a dip between two hills, urging his horse up a distant slope. They pushed their horses after him, galloping them down the side of one hill at breakneck speed, then up the side of the other. But the horses, tiring after hours of steady riding, began to blow and they had to slow them to a walk.

Cavannagh had hoped to overtake the half-breed before nightfall, but as daylight shortened and the distance between them remained the same, he despaired of catching him before he crossed into Montana.

Then it started to snow — big wet flakes falling heavily to the ground. In less than half an hour snow covered the ground. Cavannagh breathed easier, for now they could track the half-breed into the night.

Cavannagh was tired and hungry. For the past several nights he had slept only fitfully and, apart from his last strip of jerky while impatiently waiting for the field gun, he hadn't eaten all day. Jules at least had the advantage of a good night's sleep and a full breakfast.

The tracks continued in the snow. Cavannagh hoped Buffalo Johnny would camp for the night, but the half-breed kept going. For two hours they rode southward in the dark. As the hills flattened and the trees thinned, Cavannagh knew they were nearing the border. The snow lessened and changed to hard granules; the weather turning colder added to Cavannagh's discomfort. But he would not stop to either rest or eat. Despite increasing exhaustion and numbing cold, he pushed doggedly on.

Their bodies swaying and rising in their saddles with the steady movement of their horses, neither Cavannagh nor Jules spoke. One thought kept drumming through Cavannagh's mind—Buffalo Johnny! Was he as cold and tired and hungry as they?

When they arrived at a long, fingerlike coulee, they knew they had reached the border.

Jules was the first to speak.

"Well, *mon ami*, it look lak dat damn 'alf-breed get away after all."

Cavannagh didn't slow his bay's walk. "No—he hasn't."

"But d' border, *mon ami*? We no longer in d' North West Territories. We got no authority to arrest 'eem now we cross d' line. 'E know dat."

Cavannagh stopped his horse and turned in his saddle to face the *Metis*. "You're right, Jules. You go back. I'm going on after him."

"But *mon ami*, you cannat arrest 'eem."

Cavannagh turned back to his front and legged the bay forward again. Jules spread his hands in exasperation and kicked his cayuse on after his friend. "You go . . . I go," he said simply.

Cavannagh stopped his horse again and waited

until Jules caught up with him. "Go back, Jules. It's against regulations to cross the border without permission. I don't want you getting into trouble with Major Walsh."

"But you d' same, *mon ami*. You cannot arrest dat 'alf breed."

"No, I'm not the same, Jules. I'm different. I'm making my own rules. But you're going back. That's an order."

The *Metis* sat his saddle, looking back at Cavannagh in the evening's blackness, relieved by a pale moon, a skyful of glittering stars, and the snow on the ground. He wanted to stay with Cavannagh. He felt his place was beside his friend, but there was iron in the younger man's voice.

"*Oui, M'sieur,*" Jules said quietly, then pulled on the cayuse's reins, turned, and rode back across the border.

Cavannagh wasted no more time and pushed on again. After a few more miles the snow on the ground gave out and he could no longer see the half-breed's trail. But he kept riding, following the general direction his man had been going. It was turning colder and Cavannagh knew Buffalo Johnny would soon have to stop and rest. And he would have to build a fire. Out on the open prairie, Cavannagh would see it. All he had to do was keep his eyes open and his senses alert. His single-minded determination drove out the fatigue and hunger, and even dulled the numbing cold.

He stopped long enough to untie his bedroll and

wrap his blankets around his shoulders before resuming his relentless ride. Even without snow on the ground, the illumination from the pale moon and twinkling stars was enough for him to see the contours of the rolling plains. Keeping the outline of the Bear Paws over to his left, he rode generally southwest in the direction of Fort Benton.

Just as he began wondering whether Buffalo Johnny hadn't changed course to go south to the land of the Crows, he saw a flickering fire off to his front and a little to the left of where he was heading. It was no more than a quarter of a mile away.

Cavannagh rode down into a hollow, dismounted, and hobbled the bay. Then, Winchester in hand, he hurried across the hard ground toward the fire.

The realization that he was closing in on his quarry alerted his every sense. That damned half-breed must think he's safe now that he's across the border, Cavannagh reckoned as he crept stealthily forward.

When he was no more than a hundred yards away, he paused to study the scene ahead.

He could see the fire clearly, built in a slight dip below a cutbank. He was lucky he had seen it. If he had topped the rise back there a couple of dozen yards further on, he might have missed it. The fire glowed without much flame. Buffalo chips and dry grass. It would give out an intense heat after a while. But he could not see Buffalo Johnny.

Of course, Cavannagh mused, that half-Crow wouldn't be careless enough to sleep beside the fire. He was much too cunning for that. He would sleep a little beyond the fire, out of its low illumination but close enough for its warmth. Probably right up under the cutbank.

Cavannagh threw off his blanket and crept forward again, until he had covered half the distance, thankful now that the snow hadn't reached this far. Then he stopped and waited fifteen minutes, as long as he could without getting numbed from the cold, hoping to give the half-breed time to get soundly asleep.

Then he stole forward once more. Another twenty yards . . . he paused and looked carefully around . . . crept cautiously forward another ten yards, and looked around again.

There he was, under that cutbank.

Cavannagh brought up his Winchester, rose, and moved ahead, his eyes fastened onto the dark form in the shadow under the cutbank. Another ten yards. Blood pounded in his veins. A few more steps. . . . His Winchester pointed at the dark bedroll, his finger curled around the trigger.

Suddenly he heard the snick of a gun hammer. He threw himself forward just as a rifle crashed thunderously off to his left. He hit the ground heavily, rolled over once as the rifle crashed again. Swinging his Winchester up, Cavannagh fired back at the orange-red muzzle flash. His bullet caught the half-breed's rifle barrel and spun the weapon jarringly from his hands. Quick as a cat, the half-breed lunged at Cavannagh. Cavannagh caught the glint of a knife and whipped the Winchester across in front of him, catching the half-breed on the forearm, as they locked in combat.

They hit the ground together and rolled over and over, Cavannagh grabbing at the half-breed's knife arm. Again he glimpsed the glint of firelight on the arcing blade as Buffalo Johnny swung to stab him in the side of the neck. Cavannagh blocked the half-breed's wrist with his shoulder, but the knife blade dug cruelly into his upper arm. Grimacing, he reached across his chest with his right hand and grabbed Buffalo Johnny's wrist. The half-breed tried to twist the knife around to jab Cavannagh's forearm but Cavannagh pivoted on one leg and brought the other up to drive it into his adversary's testicles. Buffalo Johnny stopped it with his thigh. Cavannagh quickly changed his tactic by deftly flicking himself backward, pulling the half-breed with him and letting go.

Instantly Cavannagh sprang to his feet. Buffalo Johnny still had his knife, but as he clambered up Cavannagh kicked him, his boot catching the half-breed full in the chest. Buffalo Johnny reeled backward, dropping the knife, and as he struggled to get up again, Cavannagh smashed a balled fist into the side of his head, knocking him flying.

The wound in Cavannagh's upper left arm was bleeding. He could feel the sticky wetness running down his sleeve. He knew he had to end this fight quickly or he would be done in.

Buffalo Johnny got up again and made a try for his knife, but Cavannagh kicked it beyond his reach. Then, as fast as a striking rattlesnake, the half-breed dived for his bedroll. Cavannagh was on him an instant before he could snatch his six-gun from its holster. With a mighty heave, Cavannagh threw him across the ground, where he landed less than a foot from the fire. But with the agility of a prairie wolf, Buffalo Johnny was back on his feet, crouching, watching the tall white man through slitted black eyes.

Then slowly recognition dawned in those slitted black eyes as the glowing fire cast a light on Cavannagh's gaunt, bearded face.

Suddenly the part-Crow laughed. "Buff'lo Johnny remember you. You Mounted P'leecemans. But we in Montana. You no can take me in Montana."

"The hell I can't!" Cavannagh's one hundred and eighty pounds of bone and muscle catapulted into action. Unleashing the anger still in him, he bounded forward with a right to the half-breed's cheek that took the grin off his dark face, following with a left cross that sent his head spinning. Then two hard, fast jabs to the body. While Buffalo Johnny staggered backward, Cavannagh moved in and drove a straight right from his shoulder, catching the half-breed on the side of the nose. The half-breed landed flat on his back inches from the fire. Cavannagh sprang on top of him, rolled him over, and dragged him across the ground to his saddle. From it Cavannagh took a rawhide lariat and tied his hands and feet together behind his back.

"That'll hold you," Cavannagh panted, standing over his prisoner. A moment later he heaved him onto

231

his bedroll and threw the blankets over him.

Now the pain in Cavannagh's arm throbbed mercilessly. In a growing daze he walked the quarter-mile back to his horse, picking up his blanket on the way. Pulling himself up into his saddle, he rode back to the half-breed's camp.

Almost too tired to do anything but fall down, Cavannagh poured water from his canteen into a tin can and boiled it over the fire. Then, gritting his teeth he washed the knife wound and disinfected and bandaged it, using a field dressing from his saddlebags.

Finally he spread his bedroll on the ground and sank down into it. Exhausted, sick with pain, he was asleep in thirty seconds.

Chapter 23

Cavannagh opened his eyes slowly. It was very bright, the sun shining down from high in the sky. Where was he? Then he became aware of a throbbing pain in his left arm.

The half-breed—he had escaped!

Cavannagh sat bolt upright. Snatching his Winchester he whipped around, but the half-breed was in his bedroll, black eyes glaring hatefully at the white man.

Feeling suddenly nauseous, Cavannagh sank back into his blankets. From the sun's position he knew the time had to be close to midday. He had slept for twelve hours.

The nausea passed, its place taken by a gnawing stomach ache, and he realized he hadn't eaten for a long time. He got up. The fire had gone out, so he gathered more buffalo chips and dry grass and lit another. Then he rummaged through the half-breed's saddlebags, found jerky and tea, and boiled a can of water.

Untying Buffalo Johnny's hands, Cavannagh gave him a cup of black tea and a couple of strips of jerky.

"You break my nose," Buffalo Johnny complained

sullenly.

"You're lucky I didn't kill you," Cavannagh told him.

"What you gonna do wit' me? You no tak me to Fort Walsh. You Canadeen p'leecemans no got authority in Montana."

"You're wrong about that, Buffalo Johnny. You see, I happen to be an American citizen, and with you I've made what the law calls a citizen's arrest. That means I have to turn you over to the nearest peace officer. Well, there's no peace officer closer than the Canadian border, so when we get there I'm going to officially take you into custody as a member of the North West Mounted Police and escort you to Fort Walsh. Now hurry up and eat. We're pulling out in ten minutes."

Feeling better after chewing on jerky and drinking a mug of scalding black tea, Cavannagh broke camp and saddled the horses. Then with his pistol he prodded his prisoner up onto his horse and tied his wrists to the pommel and his feet under the animal's belly. After that he swung himself up into his saddle, gathered the reins, and legged his bay into a walk.

With no noise other than the rush of wind and the creak of saddle leather, they rode over the rolling, dun-colored prairie into a wide blue, cloud-fleeced sky. A feeling of exultation swept over Cavannagh. He had won! With the capture of this half-breed, the Colonel's gang of outlaws were no more. He had started out after this half-breed over five weeks ago, thinking he was dealing with nothing more than an outfit of whisky peddlers. Now, with a few hundred horseback and riverboat miles behind him, aided by

Dutch Schultz, Sergeant MacGregor, and Freddie Jenkins, he had smashed a ruthless, international conspiracy. He was full of the satisfaction of having accomplished something worthwhile.

Swaying backward and forward in his saddle with the movement of his horse, Cavannagh breathed deeply as he gazed around at the endless blue sky. He stared in wonder, as though seeing for the first time the fluffy white clouds decorating the heavens, with flat bottoms and varied-shaped tops, some rounded like big balls of cotton wool, others formed like huge granite-sided cliffs, and one thrusting upward like a turreted fairy-tale castle.

It came to him that he loved the freedom of these vast, lonely, wide-open prairies — from the Red to the Rockies, from the Big Horns to the Bow — so full of the excitement and challenge of life. Out here a man lived by the strength and courage of his own resources and initiative. Despite the wound in his arm and the fatigue in his body, he felt vibrantly alive.

Not even the chilling wind of approaching winter blowing down inexorably from the north could dampen his buoyancy.

ABOUT THE AUTHOR

By age six, the Australian Ian Anderson had already decided what he wanted to be when he grew up—a red-coated Canadian Mountie. By the age of seven, he also knew he wanted to be a writer.

After a brief stint with the South Australian Mounted Police where he learned to ride a horse, fight bush fires and battle with sword and bayonet, Anderson achieved his childhood goal and was duly sworn in as a loyal member of the Royal Canadian Mounted Police. His first postings were at Lethbridge, Fort Macleod, Coutts and Medicine Hat, locations which owed their historical importance to the RCMP. Anderson didn't know it then, but this was Cavannagh country! By the time Cavannagh was conceived, Anderson had had a varied career—as a Mountie in various parts of Canada, a sub-inspector in the Royal Papua-New Guinea Constabulary, and a private investigator in Melbourne. As a writer of nonfiction articles for several North American magazines, he had achieved his second objective.

Ian Anderson presently lives in Australia, where he is working on more books for "The Scarlet Riders" series.

THE NEWEST ADVENTURES AND ESCAPADES OF BOLT
by Cort Martin

#11: THE LAST BORDELLO   (1224, $2.25)

A working girl in Angel's camp doesn't stand a chance—unless Jared Bolt takes up arms to bring a little peace to the town . . . and discovers that the trouble is caused by a woman who used to do the same!

#12: THE HANGTOWN HARLOTS   (1274, $2.25)

When the miners come to town, the local girls are used to having wild parties, but events are turning ugly . . . and murderous. Jared Bolt knows the trade of tricking better than anyone, though, and is always the first to come to a lady in need . . .

#13: MONTANA MISTRESS   (1316, $2.25)

Roland Cameron owns the local bank, the sheriff, and the town— and he thinks he owns the sensuous saloon singer, Charity, as well. But the moment Bolt and Charity eye each other there's fire—especially gunfire!

#14: VIRGINIA CITY VIRGIN   (1360, $2.25)

When Katie's bawdy house holds a high stakes raffle, Bolt figures to take a chance. It's winner take all—and the prize is a budding nineteen year old virgin! But there's a passle of gun-toting folks who'd rather see Bolt in a coffin than in the virgin's bed!

#15: BORDELLO BACKSHOOTER   (1411, $2.25)

Nobody has ever seen the face of curvaceous Cherry Bonner, the mysterious madam of the bawdiest bordello in Cheyenne. When Bolt keeps a pimp with big ideas and a terrible temper from having his way with Cherry, gunfire flares and a gambling man would bet on murder: Bolt's!

#16: HARDCASE HUSSY   (1513, $2.25)

Traveling to set up his next bordello, Bolt is surrounded by six prime ladies of the evening. But just as Bolt is about to explore this lovely terrain, their stagecoach is ambushed by the murdering Beeler gang, bucking to be in Bolt's position!

Available wherever paperbacks are sold, or order direct from the Publisher. Send cover price plus 50¢ per copy for mailing and handling to Zebra Books, Dept. 1817, 475 Park Avenue South, New York, N.Y. 10016. DO NOT SEND CASH.

WHITE SQUAW
Zebra's Adult Western Series
by E.J. Hunter

Available wherever paperbacks are sold, or order direct from the Publisher. Send cover price plus 50¢ per copy for mailing and handling to Zebra Books, Dept. 1817, 475 Park Avenue South, New York, N.Y. 10016. DO NOT SEND CASH.

ASHES
by William W. Johnstone

OUT OF THE ASHES   (1137, $3.50)

Ben Raines hadn't looked forward to the War, but he knew it was coming. After the balloons went up, Ben was one of the survivors, fighting his way across the country, searching for his family, and leading a band of new pioneers attempting to bring America OUT OF THE ASHES.

FIRE IN THE ASHES   (1310, $3.50)

It's 1999 and the world as we know it no longer exists. Ben Raines, leader of the Resistance, must regroup his rebels and prep them for bloody guerilla war. But are they ready to face an even fiercer foe—the human mutants threatening to overpower the world!

ANARCHY IN THE ASHES   (1387, $3.50)

Out of the smoldering nuclear wreckage of World War III, Ben Raines has emerged as the strong leader the Resistance needs. When Sam Hartline, the mercenary, joins forces with an invading army of Russians, Ben and his people raise a bloody banner of defiance to defend earth's last bastion of freedom.

BLOOD IN THE ASHES   (1537, $3.50)

As Raines and his ragged band of followers search for land that has escaped radiation, the insidious group known as The Ninth Order rises up to destroy them. In a savage battle to the death, it is the fate of America itself that hangs in the balance!